I0734314

Voice

Diamondsong

A Concerto in Ten Parts

Part 05:
Voice

E.D.E. Bell

Atthis Arts
Detroit, Michigan

Diamondsong
Part 05: Voice

Copyright ©2019 by E.D.E. Bell
edebell.com

This is a work of fiction.
Any resemblance to actual pyrsi, winged or otherwise, is purely coincidental.

Cover Art by M.C. Krauss

Map of Ada-ji by Ulla Thynell

Interior Design by G.C. Bell

Editorial Services by:
Catherine Jones Payne, Quill Pen Editorial
Cat Rambo
M. Cusack

All rights reserved.

Published by Atthis Arts, LLC
Detroit, Michigan
atthisarts.com

ISBN 978-1-945009-45-7

Library of Congress Control Number: 2019943150

First Edition: Published July 2019

This book is dedicated to the attendees of my first reading.

Where, through laryngitis,
I read the scene with Jura in the lions' den.

To Dianne and Doreen of the Wichita Vegans.

And especially to the two gamer dudes in the audience
for encouraging me to use my voice.

Preface

Well, it was quite a spring. I'm feeling much peppier than at our last installment. Since then, we've published three wonderful books: *Five Minutes at Hotel Stormcove*, *A Spatial Surprise*, and *The Traveling Triple-C Incorporeal Circus*. The sun is warm and I'm regaining spirit.

I really just want to say how happy it makes me that you're still here reading my serial, five books in. I knew this concept was different when I started working it in January 2017, but in a world where voices were feeling very loud, it was important to me to try and write something quiet. When I'm done with *Diamondsong* I'll go back to something a bit more colorful, but this is a place I needed to be.

And if you're enjoying it, that's just . . . awesome.

Speaking of which, as always I have deep gratitude to Catherine Jones Payne. She can make the most simple of comments which cause me to do the most sleeve-rolling rewrites. This was certainly true on this volume, so I appreciate it. I'd also like to thank the otherworldly Cat Rambo for jumping in on a tight timeline, especially staying up late to finish edits right before the Nebulas! So grateful.

And to the team, I couldn't do it without you. My best thanks to Meghan Cusack, Camille Gooderham Campbell, Sasha Kasoff Moore, Laura Johnson, Deborah Reilly, and Maria Judge.

Now, sorry for that slight cliffhanger (a reference Dime would not appreciate), but I do believe Dime and Dayn just saw lamps coming toward that IC den where they'd been hiding out.

Cheers,

E.D.E. Bell

July 2019

THE WORLD OF ADA-JI

The Ja-lal: A humanoid species, dwelling in the foothills and plains of Ada-ji, characterized by broad advancements in construction, invention, and health. The Fo-ror call them brutes.

The Fo-ror: A winged humanoid species, dwelling in the forests of Ada-ji, characterized by their natural living and the use of magical powers, known as valence. The Ja-lal call them fairies.

The Ja-lal and Fo-ror are similar in form, with gray skin, but differences between them in composition and culture. Pyr is singular for a Ja-lal or Fo-ror and pyrsi is plural.

The pyrsi of Ada-ji hold many **gender identities**. While this doesn't clarify all aspects of gender, it is polite to introduce oneself with a prefix, indicating the appropriate pronouns:

Fe' indicates a set of feminine identities, using the pronouns she/her/her(s).

Ma' indicates a set of masculine identities, using the pronouns he/him/his.

Ji' indicates a set of spectrum identities, using the pronouns ve/ver/vis.

When gender is unknown, it is polite to refer to a pyr with xe/xem/xyr(s). Any group of pyrsi (plural) would be referred to with they/them/their(s).

A pyr may be generically referred to as **Burge**, short for the more formal Burgess, often for purposes of polite address or getting a stranger's attention. This is similar to the use of Sir or Ma'am on Earth. For those who hold social prejudice based on class, the term implies some sense of status or honor.

Ja-lal and Fo-ror may live up to 50 cycles. Their lives are divided into defined **epochs**, aligning with societal expectations:

Aoch	Age 0-9	Characterized by upbringing, education, and exploration
Bakh	Age 10-19	Centered on building family, performing and completing apprenticeships, and finalizing life plans
Gamh	Age 20-29	Fully immersed in their specialty or role, contributing full-time to society
Dorh	Age 30-39	Respected in leadership and/or advisory roles; it is normal to take some time for self
Eroh	Age 40+	Expected to retire and engage in craft or occasional consulting, through the **life expectancy of around 50 cycles**.

Expectations differ for each culture. For example, while a Ja-lal must develop xyr profession into a career, a Fo-ror's profession and rank are set based on xyr social class and other historical and cultural factors.

A **cycle** on Ada-ji is perhaps up to four times the length of an Earth year. So, our main character, at age 20.5 cycles, has lived more than 80 Earth years but, in relation to her life span, could be considered at the **maturity of her early forties** on Earth.

Each **turn** on Ada-ji, a period of day and then night, is **significantly longer than an Earth day**. As such, pyrsi do not sleep according to light or dark, but instead based on their own needs, lifestyle, profession, and schedule.

The Ja-lal measure time by the periodic sounding of bells; they refer to the resultant time periods with the same term. The Fo-ror are less rigid about time-keeping and refer to the equivalent time period as a span. Each **bell**, or **span**, consists of more than two Earth hours.

Smaller amounts of time are referred to by both cultures as **takes**, which can be thought of as about ten Earth minutes.

In Earth terms, it has been more than five weeks since the beginning of our tale.

The Ja-lal and Fo-ror live on separate sides of the Great Cliff. They have not interacted since the ***Great War***, an event most noted for being the **end of the Violence** on Ada-ji.

SYNOPSIS TO HERE

Fe'Diamond, known as Dime, had just left her career working for the Circles, the government of the Ja-lal. Suddenly, three hooded figures burst into her home with ropes, demanding to take her away. Without any understanding of why this had occurred, Dime and her spouse, Dayn, ran to escape them.

The intruders were revealed to be Fo-ror, commonly known as fairies. These fairies, unseen since the conclusion of the Great War, were feared and loathed by the Ja-lal, who were taught that any contact would cause the Violence to return. The fairies were said to employ a magical power known as valence, but Dime had thought this a myth—perhaps that even the fairies themselves were a myth—until she saw both herself.

Dime escaped from the city, evaded the fairies, and was rescued by a large animal species known as newts. Living amongst them, she befriended a young newt she called Juni. It became apparent to her that the Fo-ror had driven the newts from their original home, keeping them away from Fo-ror civilization with large barriers of rope netting. She was brought back to Sol's Reach by a fe'pyr familiar with fairies, Ella, who broke the news that Dime was biologically a Fo-ror—one whose wings had been removed.

After recovering, Dime traveled to the land of the Fo-ror, the Heartland, where she met the fairies Volana and Uchitar and discovered that her old coworker and flame, Rock, was being held there, in the city of Pito. She met with the High Seat, Ferala, who confessed that she was part of an old scheme to avenge the horrors of a disease called the curse, which the Fo-ror blamed on the Ja-lal. This scheme, designed by now Third Seat Neimano, was named Project Diamondsong. His plan was to remove the wings from Fo-ror newborns, place them in positions of potential influence amongst the Ja-lal, and then allow them to grow up before activating their loyalties as Fo-ror spies.

With Rock's help, Dime returned to Sol's Reach, where she visited family and friends in secret, and also snuck into the Circles' complex to find clues that would point her to potential other victims of Project Diamondsong. She was only able to locate two others: Kolk and Nafat, both of whom she informed of their history and biology to different results. Just as Dime returned to her family, the Sol's Pillars, a fringe group that believes Dime is working with the fairies, surrounded them, pursuing as they tried to leave the city.

Responding to Dime's earlier call for help, Ella arrived, followed by Juni. Tum, whose wheelchair was broken as they fled, was carried off, with everyone's concurrence, by Juni. Finally, when a pyr threatened Dime's nearly-grown child, Luja, Dime reacted subconsciously, causing a large rift in the rock that allowed them to escape. Dayn, Luja, and Ella made their way to a hiding place far from Lodon, with Dime in a continuing state of shock. There, once Dime had recovered, Ella explained that valence did not come from the wings, but from the heart. She recommended that Dime travel to the diamond caves to better learn how to use and control her powers.

Dime traveled to the diamond caves, where first, she rescued Rock. She learned to conduct valence, but almost swore off the practice when she unintentionally hurt Rock. On their way out, when confronted by Neimano, Dime decided she would not yet close that door. Upon returning to her family's hiding place, where Tum was now safe, along with Dayn and Luja, she conducted a first meeting between Ja-lal activists Ador and Hin and the Fo-ror activist Volana and her friend, Uchitar, who struggles with tzetz addiction.

The next steps remained unclear. After both parties left for their respective homes, Dime and Dayn were discussing this outside when they noticed lamps in the distance. Worrying for their family's safety once again, they decided it was time to leave.

Ada-Ji
N
E
S
W

Voice

But I am what I am.

—Murasaki Shikibu, personal writings, c1009

Act 1

A Duet

By their faces, her children already knew something was wrong. And it was hard to say it to them. Again. But she had to.

"I'm sorry. We saw lamps outside. Don't know who, but we need to go. I'll use valence to get us out, but we need to pack quickly. Please—stay quiet and do what I say."

Though it hurt her to see their resolve harden, Dime couldn't have been prouder of her children as they curtly nodded and set to packing with haste. She wasn't going to ask them to leave their items behind, especially since they'd been able to carry away so few from their home in Lodon. The lamps had been at a distance, and it was hard to move quickly over the rocky plains, especially in the dark. If they hurried, they should be able to get away, hopefully without being seen at all.

She just wasn't willing to risk a situation where the Violence could be provoked, not if she could help it. Or maybe the events outside Lodon were still too fresh in her mind: the twinkling lamps, pursuing them out across the plain. She breathed in then exhaled, trying to rid herself of the images of the pyrsi pushing each other, of their howls as they were touched with force. In either case— whatever the visitors' intent, her family needed to be on their way. She was glad that Dayn agreed.

Dime didn't have much to pack; since returning from the Heartland by way of Ella's tower, she hadn't even opened the drawers in the small room. Conditioned by the last turns of moving, she'd grown used to living out of her backpack. At least when it concerned her own items; the den's stocked supplies had provided small comforts.

So she took her notepad from the nightstand, slid her washroom items into a bag, hefted the carved owl from the center table, and walked the backpack over to the chair Ella had made her. The bag was bulging again, and Dime was barely able to fit it into the attached wooden box. Distracted, her hand scraped against the rough wood and she drew it back, wincing. She wished she could have a home again. Not an overloaded bag.

She turned to see if Tum needed help, but Luja had already been working with her, and together they were almost done gathering their things. Tum was in her chair and Agni had jumped up with her. Luja turned to Dime, holding the little dish they'd used to feed the kita. Ve held it out, hesitating.

"It's fine to take it," Dime reassured ver. "I'll settle up with the IC when there's a way to do so." She said it, remembering she wasn't allowed there anymore. Too much to parse. They needed to leave.

Luja packed the dish, as well as the bag of fermented grain that Agni liked to eat, into Tum's bag. The two moved over toward the stairway. Noting the tall closet next to them, Dime pulled out a few of the full-size tools and tied them with strands of twine to the side of her chair.

"Dayn?" She turned around, looking to see where he was.

"Ready," he said from the other room, walking out to join them. As he passed the stove and cabinets, he pushed a few more items into his bag. She hoped that included what was left of Ella's brew beans. He stopped in front of their children. "I'm sorry. We'll get through this. For now, trust your mother. Do what she says."

Still quiet, their children nodded. Dime's heart ached for what they'd endured, and her resolve only strengthened to find a way out. But, first, away from here.

"Dayn," she began, pushing her emotions back and focusing on the task at hand. "Get Tum up the stairs first. I'll lift her; you help guide. Then come back."

After a bit of confusion passed over his face, he nodded, wrapping his fingers around Tum's chair handles.

Dime took a breath, and gently lifted Tum's chair with her in it, enough that they hovered, wobbling over the ground. Dayn, not hesitating, guided her up the staircase and through the door. He returned quickly to the underground room, concern wrinkling his face for leaving Tum alone outside.

"Each of you, grab a chair."

Luja moved first. Though vis eyes were wide, ve moved to the chair ve normally used, the one by the side table, and swung it around in front of ver. Seeing vis book still on the table, ve grabbed it and tucked it away.

Dayn took vis cue, and with a shaky breath, he stood behind his own preferred chair. They both looked at Dime as if awaiting instruction.

"Last call to make sure you're not forgetting anything. If you have what you need, go to Tum." She paused. "Take the chairs with you."

Despite Dayn's clear desire to get back to his younger child, he waited as Luja bumped up the curved stairway, balancing vis bag and trying not to knock the chair against the steps or the walls. He looked back at Dime, and she nodded him forward.

Dime followed behind, taking her own chair—already loaded with her bag—and floating it in front of her as they walked up the stairs. About halfway up, she almost tripped, realizing the casual way she'd used valence to lift the heavy chair, this time without thinking of it. She breathed in, and continued up the stairwell.

"Da-da," Tum cautioned as they stepped through the door and out into the night. No question about the lamps now: several drew closer in an arc, coming from the direction of the village.

"We'll just go the other way, then." For a stride, she considered if she should just ask the visitors' intent. But they had not announced themselves; they'd not come in the openness of daylight. Instead they gathered in silence, their lamps creating an eerie arc of wavering dots.

"Maybe we should talk to them," Tum whispered.

"Yes, I was thinking the same thing," Dime responded, "but I just can't risk—"

She didn't want to finish that sentence. The idea that pyrsi would conduct the Violence wasn't new anymore. Yet she didn't want to voice it. She remembered the rift she'd made in her own fear, and tried to shake the guilt from her mind. Yet she couldn't stop seeing the pyr, howling as xyr companions sought to lift xem.

"No," Luja said, interrupting Dime's silence. "If they were here to talk, they'd announce themselves. They'd continue walking toward us and call out 'hi,' not just stand there. There'd be a pyr or two. Not a whole group. It's too *weird*."

The Aoch's candor jarred her back. Yes, they needed to leave. She'd be willing to talk, but this didn't feel like talking.

"Everyone, line up and link arms. Tum . . . will Agni stay here? Until I can return for her?" She knew how much it would upset Tum to leave the little kita at the den, but she couldn't keep her secure in flight.

"She's fine, Ma-ma. I've wrapped my scarf around her. She knows to stay close when I do that. It's how we ran with Juni. She never leaves my scarf; she knows it's safe there."

Dime still felt uneasy, but, she considered, she could hold the kita in her awareness as well. Maybe she could use valence to save her if anything happened.

Do you hear what you are saying? Oh, this was much too much pressure to put on herself. At that moment, she realized how reckless this whole idea had been—and berated herself why she'd considered it so casually a stride ago. It wasn't as if her family would be safe either, so high in the air. What if something happened to them? They needed to just stay here and deal with the visitors. Maybe it would all be fine.

She saw the lamps, drawing near. The rift flashed before her. The screams.

"Ma-ma," Luja whispered. "You can do this. Don't be scared. We believe in you."

"Just . . . just stay low," Dayn offered. "Until you feel sure."

They believe in me.

She saw the fairies standing at her door, glittering ropes in their hands. But Dime had gotten away then. Everyone was safe. They could be safe now. Her breath quivering and mind overwhelmed, Dime thought, well, she could at least try to see if they would lift. Just to try it.

Dayn wheeled Tum next to Dime, then swung his own chair beside Tum's. As he sat down, Luja moved in on Dime's other side, bumping the chair awkwardly against the ground. Ve wrapped vis arm around Dime's and it felt strong and comforting there, nothing like a ch'pyr's. Tum's hand wrapped around her as well.

Trying to calm her nerves, Dime focused again on flying. *Just like Squid the Squip,* she reminded herself, but she could not regain that sense of calm. Seeing the lights ahead, she jolted, and they all lifted into the air. Involuntarily, Luja yelped. They wobbled back and forth, and Tum began to whimper. She saw Rock's back, sliced open by the sharp stone. Her blood. The statues shattered.

I can't.

Dime set everyone down as the chairs creaked in protest. Her hands felt weak. She saw the lamps.

"Look, this was a wild idea. Let's just start walking. It's dark; they won't see us— Harm." Now the lights were definitely moving faster. Clearly, they'd seen the group lift up against the soft glow of the sky. Or heard them. Or something. Dime was starting to panic.

"Dime," Dayn whispered.

She looked over, feeling stunned.

"If they saw us, then the rumor will be there were fairies here with you."

Dime *was* a fairy. Gossip about that. "I can't control every rumor," she muttered instead. "Let's just get out of here."

"Alright, then, what didn't work there? I'm sorry, this is sort of your thing . . . I'm trying to help."

Yes, of course he was. What had it been? She felt hazy. "We felt imbalanced, and . . . wobbly. It threw me off. I can't explain it. I don't know enough. Come on, we just need to walk."

The silhouettes of pyrsi were moving into view, and now Dime could hear them talking to each other. Luja stood up and rushed over to Tum's chair, starting to push her away.

"You! Stop!" A loud voice rang out across the night, reminding her again of the Lodon mobs. She gathered herself; they had to get away.

"Leave us alone!" Dime answered. "Just a traveling family; it's no matter to you."

"You're the agent, aren't you? You're with the fairies!" They were moving closer. "Where are they? We saw them flying!"

"You don't know what you saw. Now, I've asked you to leave. Where's your sense of consent gone? Or is the Violence in charge now?" Dime was losing her temper, as flashes of the scene outside Lodon continued to interrupt her. Too recent. She shouldn't be here like this. Why couldn't they just leave her alone?

"You know their plans," another called out. "We won't let you leave. Come with us. We have a car in the village; we'll take you to Lodon, where you'll answer to the Circles."

"You'll answer to the Pillars!" another shouted. Someone started to argue with xem, and the commotion rose.

"I'm going to leave with my family now," Dime stated, her jaw beginning to tremble. "Let me leave."

"We can't," a higher-pitched voice yelled. "It's for our children now; we won't let you harm them. Or sit back while the fairies destroy us. You can't escape this time, witch."

"Come with us," another implored. "For everyone's good."

Dime could hear Tum sniffling in fear, trying so hard to be brave.

Yet now her own children had heard, with clarity, what they'd said. The Violence would be justified, they implied, if to keep themselves safe. Yet without direct cause; without clear consequence. This was how Ferala had spoken of the curse. Of the Great War. Dime wouldn't be a part of it.

"We have to stop her!" One of the pyrsi broke into a run, coming right at them.

Dime roared, throwing up a barrier between them, one made of strands of energy, glowing gold in the night. She had no idea what they were. It crackled and sparked, and the pyr backed away. She didn't think it would hurt xem, but she was glad xe hadn't tried to touch it. She needed to dismantle it as quickly as possible, once they were safe. In case it could harm. Or confuse her intent. Disorientation began to grip her again, and this time she rejected it. Urgency flooded her mind instead, and suddenly the steps were clear.

"Luja," she commanded. "Put Tum here, to face me. Tum, join my arms. I can sense Agni; I'll keep her safe. Dayn. Luja. One to each side. Pull your chairs tight and hold on."

Watching the pyrsi run around the barrier to where it ended at the den's walls, Dime realized she had no anger. Why couldn't pyrsi approach her like neighbors, ask for her explanations, talk things through? Why did they accost her in a mob? Why did they accost her at all? No, Dime did not have anger, only deep sadness that pyrsi that should be working together had decided instead to divide. Dime would help fix it, if she could. But not like this.

The sadness calmed her, steadied her, as she grasped Tum's smooth arms. And she imagined, in the flash of time that she had, what that would be like if pyrsi were all willing to talk. To learn. And with a spark of hope as golden as the shield before her, she knew they would get there. She believed.

But not from here. Not tonight.

She closed her eyes and, together, Dime and her family lifted into the air. There was no teetering or wavering, and with calm, she dismantled the barrier below, releasing the energy she'd used into small sparks, darting through the night and offering themselves to anyone interested in accepting them. Into each, she implanted a single word: *Listen*.

Everyone was silent now: Dayn, Luja, Tum, Agni, herself, as they rose high and the plains spread below them, the den no longer visible. That den, she was certain, now filled with pyrsi rummaging through it for clues of her destination.

To hide that destination, she set out in the wrong direction, slowly curving around. Even in the dark, she had a sense now where Ella's home was. It drew her like a wind rope, back to a place of safety.

But she didn't go there, either. She wouldn't endanger Ella any more than she already had. And Ella's tower was too close to the edge, too approachable. No, she'd go somewhere they wouldn't look, not anytime soon.

She was tired by the time the treetops of the old woods poked into the distance. And without light or any knowledge of the land around her, she leaned deeply into her pendant, to sense each tree and rocky ledge, and guide her family down onto an area that seemed habitable. Water, room to build. And a view of Sha.

Weary, she set everyone down into the small clearing. Then opened her eyes.

Dime felt like they'd disconnected from the world those next bells. Not wanting to explore in the darkness, they nestled in amidst the three-leaf. There, as Dime breathed in the calming musk of the woods, Dayn gently stroked the soft layer of hair across her scalp until she fell asleep.

When Sol rose, though its rise was subtler here in the woods, they worked to erect a small shelter, as best they could without the aid of stone blocks or prepared stonemix. Dayn's construction expertise came in almost as handy as Luja's youthful strength; Dime watched with astonishment as her child, sleeves rolled to vis shoulders, heaved long trunks, and sawed them with the tools she'd grabbed from the den. Eager to help, Tum tirelessly wove panels from strands of tall shrubs, stacking them to one side for when the structure was ready.

Dime used her valence, finding its practice more comforting than she had before. She eased into it, in this secluded place, away from the pressures of the world for a while, and not thinking anyone would be able to detect the small amount that she used. Even if Ja-lal could sense valence, which she didn't know, it was unlikely that pyrsi would be close enough, given the superstition they held for the woods. If any Fo-ror were looking for her, they'd have no reason to look here. Her confidence grew, as she helped move felled trunks and lift trimmed beams into place.

Yet she worried as daylight passed, bell after bell. She needed to be out there, doing something, not hiding in the woods where her family had to live without a proper food supply and without plumbing. As serene as it was to build this makeshift home and listen to the wind rushing through the trees, it was not her life. It was not helping to stop the tearing of the world outside. Let alone mend it.

Needing a break, she left—a quick flight in her chair—to let Ella know the latest, but Ella was not at home and no note had been left outside her locked door.

So she returned. Not seeing anyone for the moment, she lay back along the rough bench Dayn had built and admired the sloped, but solid, shelter. And she was not surprised when he joined her, nudging her over so he could sit. He rested a hand on the top of her boots.

"What's your plan?" he asked.

As comforting as it was to see him, Dime felt frustrated, somehow, that he'd asked what the plan was, rather than whether she even had one. Or whether he could help to develop one. Knowing this frustration was not Dayn's fault, she tried to answer both questions as though they were the same.

"I've only concluded a few things."

He waited.

"I can't hide anymore. I've said it again and again, yet here I am in a burrow of my own." She sat up, her gaze sweeping across the rich blue strip of Sha that was visible through the clearing. "And I need to speak. Volana said that, over and over, and I've been thinking about it. Voice. Pyrsi need voice. Hiding. Voice. It all seems related." A bird cawed from above, and she turned to find it, but instead only saw a wavering branch.

"Do you know where you're going to go?" Dayn asked. "No offense to your accommodations, but the rest of us are not eager to travel by flying chair-chain too terribly often. I mean, we will if we need to."

Being honest, Dime hadn't thought as much about where she needed to go. There were some obvious choices, and she hadn't mulled too much about them. The idea that had stayed on her mind was more one of numbers.

"Not really. I'm more worried about being alone." Turning to Dayn, she rested a hand on his knee. "No! I know I'm not alone—I have the best friends in Ada-ji. What I meant," she corrected, "is this continued idea that everything that's happening is centered around me. I'm the focus or the victim or the catalyst or something, but freedom is about all of us. Voice is about all of us. I don't want that to get lost."

Dayn paused. "I'm not exactly sure I understand."

"I mean, whatever way there is to bring pyrsi together, we need lots of others with us. It shouldn't rest on any one pyr. It can't."

"Right. No, I get that part. What I didn't understand is . . . isn't that what you've done already? Joining with the Free Winds. Bringing in Volana and Uchitar. Connecting to the Foundry—isn't that what Volana called her group?"

Dime nodded. Realizing he hadn't seen her, she added, "Yes.

Foundry." She scooted to an angle, thinking about what he'd said. "Well, sure, ok. Then we need more of that. We need to spread this message. So, I guess if the question is 'where should I go,' the way to get there is 'who do I need to bring in next?'"

This idea took her in several directions, but one continued to pop up front of the others. Not a group or a coalition, but the single-most powerful pyr to which she hadn't yet spoken. *Sala.*

Yet Dayn still worked for the Circles, at least if he could convince them of the necessity of his extended absence. Dime was surely on the outs there, but could she continue to shatter the structures that held Dayn's life as well? He was here, after all. She supposed she ought to just ask him.

"I was thinking about talking to Sala."

She wasn't sure why he grinned.

"Of course you were," was all he said.

"What about your career? In the CC? I don't want to—"

She didn't really appreciate that Dayn burst out laughing.

"I'm sorry!" He placed a hand on her upper arm, giving it a squeeze. "I'm sorry! It's just . . . you think my plan is to *go back to work?* Dime. Love. Look around. We didn't build a literal hut in the forbidden dark woods so we could stay here a couple of bells."

She didn't enjoy his tone, and seeing her irritation, he softened it.

"Hey, this has been stressful for all of us. We've cut you a lot of slack, cut us some too."

He was right, she knew. She tried to shake off the last piece and return to the point. "Alright. Well, then I won't worry about all of that for now. And I think I should talk to Sala."

She paused, waiting for him to caution her or suggest alternatives. He didn't. "So, the Boring Project. We were talking about it,"—she didn't want to bring up the situation at the den, but they'd been discussing it before they saw the lamps—"and I'm not sure if we finished. Anything else you can tell me before I go would probably help."

Though tensing at this topic, he tapped a stick against the

ground, listing off whatever details he could. "The whole thing was intended to be exploratory science. Find out what's in the rocks, what could be safely mined, and just understand the composition better. In case there were better opportunities for structures underground, maybe to increase water flow or find new water sources to aid the villages.

"We didn't have the information to do much of that safely, but understanding the makeup of Sol's Reach was one of the goals. I mean, that's science. Learn what you don't know. We had a few serious mishaps early on, which is why they'd backed off and started to exercise more caution."

She hated to confirm this, but wanted to be clear. "And you never heard one mention of the Heartland, diamonds, or even drilling to the sur."

"I did not," he said.

Dime rubbed her own temples. "There's so much out there to understand. It's too much for any pyr."

Dayn drew his arms around her. "Well, isn't that just why you were saying we need to work together?"

She leaned in, allowing herself to absorb the warm comfort of his embrace.

When Dime found ver, Luja was staring out at the Sha.

"It's beautiful, isn't it?" she offered. "The way the light sparkles off the crests? The pure color and shine? The . . . expanse."

Luja nodded.

"I wanted to ask you something. In case it comes up."

"Sure."

Sometimes that was about all the answer one could expect from an Aoch. Sometimes they wouldn't stop. Dime tried not to grin. "If someone is suffering of tzetz, how would I treat them?" Since it was sort of obvious, there was no need to tiptoe around it. "For Uchitar. I found him once, unresponsive, and didn't know what to do. I thought . . . I should understand better. Just in case. I mean, Volana is staying with him now, trying to help. So maybe he'll be fine. I'm sure he will."

Luja turned around, with a sarcastic tilt of the face that indicated vis clear belief that Dime was incredibly naïve. "Maybe. It's a very addictive thing, Ma-ma. I hope he's clear from it, but you can't assume. Not for many cycles. If ever."

"Why do pyrsi start it?" she wondered aloud.

"Maybe be grateful you don't have a reason to know." Luja flinched and glanced away. "Sorry. The way pyrsi talk about it is important too, is all I meant. In addition to understanding it. I mean, I get it's just us here."

If Luja thought ve'd been rude, Dime didn't take it that way. She was surprised by the wisdom coming from her child. And impressed. "Good point."

She turned away, suddenly feeling too awkward to see the equally surprised look she knew Luja was giving her.

"So, when you say treat him," ve said, "it depends on his state. If he's actively using, you mostly need to keep him out of trouble and let the tzetz work through his system. Make sure he didn't have too much; too severe of a drop-off could kill him. You'd give him as much water as he'll tolerate, and try introducing calming foods, like bread. If he's withdrawing, you need to help him expel his stomach, while still administering enough water so he doesn't dehydrate. And if he's craving more, well, that depends on the situation. It's the hardest treatment of any of them."

Dime was curious what ve meant by that, but she remembered something else. "What if he's unconscious? Or asleep? Or you don't know which?"

"You should be able to tell unconscious from asleep. If xe's asleep and breathing fine, you could keep an eye on xem." Dime noticed ve was no longer talking about Uchitar in particular. "If something doesn't seem right, try waking xem. If xe doesn't wake, truly, the best thing is to find a medic. But if you don't have a medic, then make sure xe is breathing and xyr heart is beating. If it is, just turn xem on xyr side and keep an eye on xem until you can get help."

"What if xe isn't? Breathing right? Or xyr heart?"

Luja did vis best to show Dime how to induce breathing. "As for the heart, much more complicated. Sometimes massage helps. But usually, we whisper to xem. Try to get xem to hear us and restart."

"That works?"

"Sometimes. I've ... been studying it. Ma-ma?" Luja leaned forward, urgency in vis eyes. "I'm going to make pyrsi better. I'm going to discover new methods and make pyrsi's lives easier."

Dime tried not to let the tears form in her eyes. Not because she was ashamed of them, but because she didn't want them to cloud the pride. "Buttons. I know you will."

As Dime packed again, ready to leave for Lodon, she did consider the irony of how recently she'd escaped the city not once, but twice, and now she was going back.

But it was different now. Now she had valence and knew how to use it. Now her children were safe. *Now I'm already an outlaw. Now they can deal with me.* "When I said no more hiding, I meant it," she said.

"Good for you!" Dayn responded with a grin.

She started, more than embarrassed he'd been standing right there.

"Your hair is kind of cute," he said, appearing to change the subject.

"Thanks." She ran her hands through the short layer, wondering when she'd need to style it. She wondered if it would curl; she'd noted a variety of textures among the Fo-ror. "I may just be growing it to be stubborn."

"A little stubborn never hurt anyone."

"What about a lot stubborn?"

"That depends." He grinned again.

Dime was glad to see some spirit back to him. They'd always been friends, enjoying life together and laughing at its quirks. Life had become so serious lately. She leaned in for what was meant to be a short kiss, but turned into one a bit more involved. They pulled away, and seeing his eyes sparkling at her, she caressed the side of his cheek. She returned his playful glance, knowing what he was thinking about. They'd flown together to a lower ledge a while back, where avoiding the sharp rocks had been a challenge but the view had been terrific. Perhaps valence wasn't so bad after all.

"Well, I'm off to the city," she said, glad that without the need to pack for a longer trip and with Rock's owl gracing their little shelter, her bag was considerably lighter.

"Yes, well, give 'm Dime."

"What does that mean?" She laughed.

He offered her a tight embrace. "Only you can say."

No matter how many turns had passed, Dime still wasn't used to living outside the regiment of the city bells, so it was jarring to hear them again from the distance, like a return to real life. By her estimate, there were only a few daytime bells left before Sol set back into night. Hoping to return to the hut, as Tum had dubbed it, before dark, she flew faster than she had before, and even Dime was surprised how quickly the towers of Lodon rose before her, the gleam of their gold accents especially pretty in the late-day light.

"Home," she whispered into the wind.

Betting that no one would be staring up into the brightly glowing sky, she moved quickly and stayed away from windows as she zig-zagged her way toward the height of the city. The air pushed against her face, and she relaxed into the sensation, which gave her a sense of freedom.

Yet, now used to old woods trees and Ella's four-story home, she shuddered at the idea of flying all the way to the top of the Circles complex. Besides, that would reveal her valence, something she definitely wasn't ready to do. She would stroll on in the old way, and they could try to stop her.

Previously, she'd feared defying the Circles' orders—no one did that—or even receiving a hemsa for disobedience. She was over it now. And so, stowing her chair and bag in the back of a corner garden, she proceeded to walk up the curved path toward the complex. The worn stone pavers felt familiar against the soles of her boots, and, once, she closed her eyes just to absorb the sounds of the city: the low churning of toothcars and the distant clatter of construction.

Of note, there were considerably more banner ads for Spicy Sandwich as she rounded the bend, and, apparently, a new location down the street. She hoped things were going well, a little sad she couldn't just stop in. No hullnut, but the marinated greenpulp with red chilies and fried beancube sounded excellent. But that was a favor they didn't need.

Two pyrsi were stationed per door as she approached the rounded entrance way of the complex, its sculpted towers rising endlessly above. "Hello," she said as they gasped and stepped to block her way. "I'm Fe'Diamond—I'm here to see the Light. If she's in?"

"The . . . Light?" The guards cut each other a glance.

"Yes," Dime confirmed. "Light Sala. I'd like to talk to her, if she's willing."

They stood there, looking like they hoped she'd take it back. Finally, one answered. "Is the Light . . . expecting you?" Noting the disturbance, a few of the nearby pyrsi turned in place, as if wanting to do something to help, but not sure what.

Well, good, it seemed Sala was in. It would have been a bit anticlimactic to have to come back. "No, she's not. But I'm hopeful she'll want to talk—if you could just let her know I'm on the way up. Thanks!"

Seeming to forget they'd been trying to block her, the guards actually stepped aside by instinct as Dime strode through. Realizing she wasn't going to stop, a few raced ahead of her, moving their arms in nonsense ways as she passed them a second time.

For the most part, Dime ignored the whatsleft stew of reactions as she ascended each section of the tower. Gasps, dropped papers, and outright squeals joined whispers and hurried steps, while Dime continued to stroll, appreciating the architecture and design of the towers as she never had before. Little details, like the scrollwork on a column, or a small inlaid ledge. She imagined all the artists who had crafted these elements, and the cycles of pyrsi who'd walked here before. And this time, instead of walking under the archway to the IC, she continued on through the large upper atrium, to the entrance to the central complex tower, with its broad golden domes and peaks.

She was expecting some type of argument, but instead a Light's attendant was waiting for her, xyr arm across xyr chest in a salute. Xe fanned xyr fingers at Dime's approach.

"Hello," Dime said with a nod and a fan of her own fingers.

"Welcome, Burgess Diamond. Please, the Light is expecting you."

Dime did feel the sting of the omission of her previous title, however proper, but it was quickly replaced with the amusement that they had reversed the element of surprise. Yes, of course, Sala was now waiting for *her*. That was fine.

"I am honored to answer her request," Dime responded, unconcerned by whatever proprieties they wanted to issue. She wasn't here for her ego. If she were driven by ego, she would have— No, no use rehashing that. She followed the attendant as they wound up and around the tower.

Bravado aside, it was a bit surreal to walk up the narrow stair, ascending through the floor of the gold-trimmed office of the Light, a round room surrounded by huge, geometric windows and striped by rainbows from the exceptionally large beveled panels of glass. The view was unimpeded by walls or tower spikes or stoves or halls, and somehow, the mountains seemed to loom closer here. Dime could have stared out over the city forever, and she could only imagine what views of Sol's rise and set were enjoyed in this unique space: the peak of the whole city.

She'd never been in the Light's private office before—there was no question that's what this was—but even she was surprised to see an actual gold desk. Even Ferala hadn't gilded his whole desk, she thought. Certainly it was only gilded.

"Thank you. I'd like to speak to her alone," Sala said.

With a deep salute and troubled eyes, the guard left, descending back into the floor and closing the door—Dime figured a door in the floor was still called a door—above xem. She looked back at the leader of the Ja-lal, a low Dorh, younger than Ella, but, she supposed, not too far from Ador's age. As always, the fe'pyr was impeccably dressed and fashioned, with a brightly-hued tailored suit, and tattoos boasting all levels of rank and accolade. She offered a measured smile.

"Diamond. Thank you for joining me."

"Thank you for having me. And you can call me Dime."

Sala rose from her seat and moved over to where Dime stood. Between Sala's platform shoes and Dime's own petite height, Dime was forced to look substantially upward to avoid talking to her leader's chest.

"Dime. Your hair, is it a statement?" Sala asked.

That's right. She'd so been expecting the whispers and stares she'd received, she forgot how strange she must look here with her low crop of hair. It wasn't as if Dime could see herself; sometimes she even forgot it was up there. But a statement? No, she wasn't— *Oh.* Now that she considered it.

"Somewhat." Dime ran her hands through it, unused to its

prickly softness. She wondered if that was rude. None of the Fo-ror had been touching their hair.

"It conceals you," Sala said, walking in a slow circle around her.

But, yes. Dime hadn't even thought through all the implications of a covered scalp in Sala's eyes. And it irritated her that Sala had gone right to it. Maybe they could have caught up a bit before she implied Dime's criminality. After all her cycles here—had she suddenly expected something different?

"Your clothes—" Dime pointed to Sala's custom-designed and pyrsonally-branded suit, with touches of her signature yellow but also elements of black and subtle hints of frost. "They are most certainly a statement, if an absolutely striking one, and they conceal you as well. Character. Concealment. Revelation. They are part of all of our presentation. If that's wrong, why not just walk around naked?"

Dime knew she should be more formal in Sala's presence, more concerned about what she said, but in a strange way, Sala was the most familiar thing she'd seen in a long time. Work. Home. Authority. Her old boss' boss, really. Probably a third boss in there; it wasn't always clear.

Sala's eyes widened a touch, then narrowed back. "Will you tell me what happened? That turn?"

"Yes." She took a breath. Talking about that turn always agitated her, but it was a reasonable question. "I left my going away party and carted home my crate of office stuff. I was starting to put it all away. Out of nowhere, representatives of the Fo-ror arrived to take me back to their government, for my connections to the IC and knowing that I had just left." She didn't want to divulge all that she'd learned about Neimano and the Seats, but she knew Sala would expect a reason why it was Dime they'd sought.

"I didn't know anything about that part at the time, and these strange pyrsi had just shown up without permission, so I said no. Their government is as used to hearing 'no' as this one is, so it didn't go over great, and they moved to take me with them . . . without my consent. But I got away.

"I wanted to come home, back to my city, but Sol's Pillars told everyone I was some sort of traitor, since they wanted everyone to stay scared. I was scared and unsure myself. So I stayed away."

"You didn't." Sala waved her hand as if Dime were obviously here. And without doubt she knew about Dime's previous visit, when she'd walked inside wearing sandwich ads, accessed the IC records section, and then run from the tower like a bumbling ch'pyr. But Dime had been talking about at first and in general, and she wasn't ready to tell Sala about her initial trip to the Heartland—where she actually had walked around naked, now that she remembered it.

"Oh, right. Well, the first time, I wanted to find my family. As you can imagine, they were very worried about me, as I was about them." She realized she didn't know much about Sala's family. Sala wasn't currently married and didn't have children, to her knowledge, but she didn't know how she kept her company. "And as for now, I've had more time to think. And I'm not running or hiding anymore."

"Thank you." Sala barely tipped her chin. "For coming back. We'll need you to stay here. I'll assign someone to take the information that you have."

Stay here? "No, sorry. I'm not here to submit to the Circles. I'm here to talk to you about something serious. A few things, really, but one I know you have direct power to stop."

"You'd disobey a direct order?" A direct order *from the Light* was implied. "That's a crime."

Yes, Dime knew. Did they have to go right to this again? She had come here to try and help; maybe Sala could recognize that. But then, what had changed for Sala? Everything had changed for Dime. If that wasn't yet obvious, maybe she just needed to tell her. "The moment I was forced out of Lodon by mobs and without any protection from the Circles, I decided I was no longer bound by its laws. I'm a citizen of Ada-ji. And as Ada-ji has no government yet, I'll just answer to myself. To Sol. To Sha. However you'd like to say it."

Sala shook her head, letting a huge sigh. Dime noticed that she seemed to drop her airs, deflating back to the look of any normal pyr. "Why didn't you come to us in the first place?"

Sure. Sala would never consider someone not viewing the Circles as the center of the world. Didn't Dime just explain that to her? Dime snorted, not meaning to. But she did. "I don't *trust* the Circles anymore, Light Sala. Is that my fault? Or the Circles'?"

"What about your spouse?"

There it was. She'd already decided she wasn't dealing with that, and she had Dayn's blessing as well. Her voice did tense a bit. "Don't threaten my spouse, Sala, or you'll make my point. We have a new career now, which is preventing *the Violence* from returning. Yes, I said it. I'll say it again. The Violence is real and it's looming over Ada-ji. And if Fo-ror and Ja-lal voices continue to pick at each other and scare regular pyrsi who don't have a broader sense of things, its return is exactly what's going to happen. And to Dayn and me, preventing the Violence is way more important than our social or civic standing."

In the ensuing silence as she recovered some calm, Dime realized she was being terse with someone who had every reason and authority to order her out, while Dime hadn't yet been able to have the conversation they needed to have. She offered an apologetic smile. "Light Sala. I'm not here against you. I'm with you."

Sala twitched. "What about the Fo-ror?"

Dime knew this answer meant the world, so she looked Sala right in the eyes. If at a considerable angle. "I'm with them too."

Sala's lips pulled tight, before she finally responded. Now Sala's voice was the one growing tense. "You don't understand. You're against the Violence? Then you should be against them. You should be begging to help the Circles, whatever way you can." Her expression soured. "You have no idea. Their *valence* . . . where do you think the word came from? Their *valence* almost destroyed all of us! And it could again."

She believed that, actually. Her pendant pulsed against her chest, as if it had heard. But why had the Fo-ror been so scared?

What machinery and blades had the Ja-lal threatened them with, to push things so far? How could she know, when all the records had been hidden or destroyed? Dime didn't know where all the blame lay, but she knew enough that she was no longer interested in one-sided deflections.

"Did you hear what happened outside of the gates?" Realizing she'd crossed her arms, she uncrossed them. "Or did you get some report that said I broke into the city, rifled through some records, then stirred up a protest?"

Sala's expression answered that.

"The Violence broke out. Not from the Fo-ror. From you. The Ja-lal. Your impassioned burgesses, so worried about some pyr they know *nothing* about, began to argue. Since the Circles tell them what to think, they aren't used to arguing. And when they couldn't agree, they started pushing each other with their hands and shouting harsh words. Then—my child. They put their hands on ver, just for trying to leave."

It was clear Sala was troubled by her words. Good. Maybe she was here for trouble. But no, she was here for a reason. "I'm sorry, it's hard to think about." She closed her eyes a moment, collecting herself. "Oh, and I compromised IC den 3-17 and took some supplies. Sorry. But there's a specific reason I'm here now." Better to get there. She took a breath. "I beg you, Light Sala, please stop the Construction Circle's Boring Project until you can reassess its goals."

The taller fe'pyr threw up her arms, hiding no incredulity on her face. "What? Construction? Science? Why would I stop that?"

"Sala. Please. Listen to me. The machines aren't in the mountains. They're sur, near Fo-ror lands. They are drilling into the rocks there, over a series of caves. They may crack the surface of Sol's Reach, disturb the water flow . . . destroy Pito." Dime was so certain Sala knew what Pito was that she didn't bother to explain. "It would be the Ja-lal bringing the Violence then. The Ja-lal restarting the Great War. Did you order that? Either way, please—stop it.

For a while, anyway, until you learn more. Send the IC out, survey their locations. Then decide. If it's just exploratory, there can't be anything so urgent you can't pause until you know more."

Returning to her chair, Sala rested her elbows on the gold desk, and seemed to be thinking, as if Dime weren't even there. Was she dismissed? She doubted it. Sala was used to others' time not being important. Dime didn't care; in fact, she'd stay as long as she needed to convince her. She glanced around the room. At least Ferala had offered her a chair. Ok, stool. But still.

"If you stop," Dime offered, "if you take a step back and call for discussion, there are others who will support you."

Sala seemed surprised, as if she'd forgotten Dime was there. "I'm the Light," she snapped. "I don't need support. I already have support. You're the one disturbing it."

Of course. She equated introducing discussion with disturbing order. Undeterred, Dime continued. "Sol's Pillars aren't as powerful as you worry. Even now. Dangerous, but not yet powerful. For now, they're just loud. But that's the thing—they're speaking. We should be speaking too. The Circles. Individuals. The Free Winds . . . I know it's a touchy subject, but the Free Winds are not enemies of the Circles. They are only trying to progress its thinking, to offer new ideas. Their leader, Ador, I know him well, and—"

"You know Ador?"

Dime couldn't read the twisted expression on Sala's face, and she wondered if Ador had understated his level of petitioning to power.

"I do. I know Ador well. I've spoken to him about all of this. And to a group of Fo-ror, with similar aims. And if you and High Seat Ferala could just speak, even in private, you could—"

"What did you say?"

Dime wasn't used to being interrupted like this, but she supposed, neither was the Light. And perhaps mentioning Ferala had been a step too much. Well, too bad. She was tired of secrets.

"Yes, the Fo-ror leader. I've spoken to him also. What, you think

I'd only go here? That I've done nothing else these last turns? I'm sure you know; his name is Ma'Ferala. I talked to him. I had questions, as you can imagine. I certainly wanted to know why they'd burst into my home. So I talked to Ferala. I found him . . . decent. Just as I know you to be decent. I don't see why you can't just get together and—"

"Where did you—"

"Please! Let me speak. I'm not the point here. I talked to Ferala and I'm talking to you because pyrsi respect you. I worked here, remember? Pyrsi think highly of you. There are grumbles, there are always grumbles, but they respect you and look up to your leadership. They'll listen to you. Why can't you listen to me, when you must have some sense of what I've seen? Would I petition you on a whim? After all those cycles in the IC, keeping my respectful distance and doing my job, do you think I suddenly don't know what I'm talking about? I'm suddenly mindless because we disagree? Why can't you trust me, just a little? Why can't you stop the Boring Project before it restarts the Great War? Why can't you talk to Ferala? He seems worried. Maybe you're worried too. Just talk to each other. Come up with a plan."

Sala rose to her feet. "We *have* a plan and you're destroying it." Her eyes twitched and she turned toward a window. "*We* don't have a plan; I didn't mean that. I've never met the High Seat." Dime believed her; she couldn't imagine Sala lying outright.

"What I mean," Sala continued, "is that it is imperative that our cultures remain apart. That's how it's been for ages and how it needs to stay. The details of the Great War . . . it was devastating. Horrific. The Violence at every turn. You think I don't understand that? You should be grateful that you don't!

"And, no, not just in the past. Here, you lecture me about the Violence like I've never seen it. Like I can't imagine it. Reports of the Violence—who do you think sees them? Who administers the hemsa, keeps tabs on severe offenders? Some agent?

"Burgess *Diamond*, I know what the Violence can do. What it has done. And no matter what you've been through, I don't see who you possibly are to barge in here, treat me like some drinking friend, and tell me to cease unrelated Circles programs and jaunt down to Pito to chat with your friend, High Seat Ferala. Fe'pyr, are you *listening* to yourself?"

Sala walked back to the front of the desk and lowered her voice. "I know the Violence isn't gone. The Violence was never gone. Do you think I'm naïve? That I hide under this desk and take dalcakes? Of course the Violence isn't gone. It's my job—my job—to keep it out of sight, so pyrsi can live safe, happy lives. And that's not as fun of a job as you may think, especially when everyone out there just wants to tell me how I'm doing it wrong."

The Boring Project was not unrelated; she'd just explained that. She knew Sala was frustrated, and she was frustrated too. Dime had not wanted this conversation to be so heated, but she just couldn't see dancing around what could amount to pyrsi's lives. Maybe she'd come across as too condescending. Falling off a cliff, being turned into an outlaw, and losing your home could do that. Having to relive what she'd seen like it was a note of curiosity. But she was also tired of being treated like she'd never had a career herself. Like she hadn't been one of the very pyrsi chosen to ensure the protection Sala now described.

Dime wasn't *no one*. And she was tired of powerful, wealthy leaders lecturing her how difficult their lives were while they sat, unperturbed, in offices any other pyr could dream to even visit. Maybe it wasn't her place to say any of that; she didn't know. But Sala was continuing.

"And this Ferala, he's doing the same thing. Don't you see that? He's protecting his pyrsi and I'm protecting ours. And all you are doing is causing chaos, running around, and getting in our way. The Violence at the gates of Lodon? Harm in a basket, Dime, now I have to calm that as well? You're disrupting, not helping."

Sala clasped her hands together, in a conciliatory gesture. "Come. This has been difficult for us both. Let me host you here.

You'll be treated well. We'll bring your family. We'll keep you away for a while. I'll announce you're in custody. Or gone. Or anything you want. Pyrsi will forget. They'll go back to their lives. Please."

Great sadness weighed on her as she considered Sala's words, and drank in their kind and pleading tone. Her eyes held no deceit; only a genuine concern. As if the confinement she offered were a generosity. Dime had to remember that—each pyr had their own perspective, and no one else should define that for xem. They'd all been entrenched here.

Yet Dime wasn't going to stay. She didn't want to deny her request yet; there was more to discuss, and denying Sala could cross a line that would lead to open defiance. And unlike the tenuous scene in the offices of the Seats, there was no time pressure here, no hovering guards. Sala seemed content to give her whatever time she needed. But of course it wasn't the same. This was *home.*

Then, what else did she need to say? Dime paged through all the thoughts she'd had on her way here, but it was as though they'd been dropped into a bin. What was important?

"Light Sala, I've talked to the Fo-ror. Not the jerks who accosted me, but others. I've spent time talking to them, trying to understand. It's not like we're taught. They're not even that different, at least not at their core. Their valence—you seem to fear it above all else." A pang struck her, knowing pyrsi would fear her too, if they knew. "Yet it's natural, a strength, you could say, that a pyr projects out onto the world around them. It should be feared no more than any part of a pyr.

"Yet, Ja-lal are strong, as well. They deny that strength, largely, hide it. They've learned to focus inward. Resolve, courage—look what we've done. Look at this beautiful city, and the pyrsi living in health and harmony within it." She grimaced. "At least they were. And they can again."

"What are you implying?"

Dime's eyes met Sala's, and Dime realized how entirely much she simply missed the truth. If she wasn't going to hide anymore, then the truth shouldn't have to either. "The Ja-lal have valence too."

Sala jolted in place, but Dime kept on.

"It grows inside of them. Some have likely used it, concealed it. Most deny it, let it wither, because our fear has developed into full-blown ignorance. I wonder, Sala, if we dislike them or ourselves."

Sala wavered, just slightly. "These words are a crime."

"No, Sala, these words are my truth. What I know to be true, what I don't yet know, and my thoughts about both. The Ja-lal valence does not move objects, does not impact the external. But there is something substantial to it, something we have yet to understand."

The Light stepped forward and stood an arm's width from Dime, towering over her. She had to admit this rattled her. A lot.

"You're so righteous, aren't you?" Sala's face was so close. "Have you listened to yourself? I'm the one pyr who could save you, and you've been rude from the moment you walked up here. I'm trying to be understanding because I can only imagine you've been through a great deal. But you have no right. And this last piece *cannot* be true and it *cannot* be spoken. Don't you see that?"

The idea of needing *saving* when she'd done nothing wrong rankled her, but moreso, she saw Sala's pain as well. Tangible frustration crossed between them, like crackles of lightning. Here was someone with tremendous burdens placed on her every turn, alone, here in a tower, which now that Dime considered it, felt lonely.

Dime relaxed her posture, widening the space between them. "Light Sala, I'm sorry for any tension I've created. I'm not trying to be rude, and I understand the last turns have been difficult for us both. But since then, I've traveled over a great deal of Ada-ji, I've talked to pyrsi, and I've seen both cultures—their desire for peace and harmony as well as their willingness to ignite over ignorance and entitlement. Maybe I got us off to a bad start here, but I'd really like to talk."

"What do you think this is?" Sala waved an arm, but backed a few steps further away. She rolled her eyes.

Dime took a calming breath, knowing she was a stride from losing patience. "I said we should talk. This isn't talking. This is some kind of . . . theater show. And I just tried to tell you, I'm sorry if I'm contributing to that. What I'm suggesting is we get a tea, settle in, and you let me talk about what I've seen. I think that if you hear the specifics of the Boring Project, you'll realize you need to do something before hundreds of pyrsi are killed. And—"

"Do you think you can speak to me like that?"

Dime closed her eyes. This wasn't going how she intended. But how was anyone supposed to have a conversation when half the ideas were too criminal to even suggest? And when every honest thing Dime tried to convey was taken as some sort of affront. These topics upset Dime, and yeah, maybe she wasn't focused on her etiquette while discussing them. It was the Circles' preconceptions and long-standing lack of challenge that were the issue here, not Dime. Not honesty. Not the truth. She opened her eyes again.

"I am trying to tell you the truth, even things I'm not sure I should be. And I understand that I am just some pyr, intruding on your shift. I was hoping we could talk."

Sala flung her hands forward, curling her fingers. "Stop. Just *stop* that. Do you think I don't know who you are? That you're some stranger?" Sala walked over to the window, not looking at Dime anymore.

"I was going to select you, Agent. I'd heard nothing but good from anyone I respect. I was watching you with great interest for IC Chief. For my own Circle. Do you know what it's like to have the rug slip from under you? To look like a fool? When that pyr, who you thought you could trust, who everyone said was amazing, abandons her duties and is now a Sol-blessed outlaw? Who's had her head filled with fairy dreams and doesn't understand the realities of the world? Now who do I pick? For the IC. No one in their leadership has half the skill you do, half the patience, half the caring."

"Rock does."

"What?" Sala spun around. "Agent Rock? Are you serious?"

"Do I look like I'm here to make jokes? Yes. Agent Rock. She's the best harmed agent I've ever met, and if you didn't see that, then fire your managers, because they're hiding it from you for their own gain. Start with Atti. He's a bully and beyond that, a total dungstink. I get it. He's messed up too. He needs therapy or something. That's what they all say. Then get him some Solharmed therapy, and don't impose his problems on everyone else."

"Atti comes from an excellent family, Dime. I've dealt with his father for—"

"An excellent family?" Dime could feel her control slipping again and she knew her time here was about done. But she wasn't feeling like stopping either.

"An excellent family? You mean like Hara? For whom I had to do turns of paperwork and explaining for not hiring her little prize of a nephew, who was lazier than sweetsap? Then what about Toug? She doesn't do anything. And she's so delusional about it no one wants to be the one to look her in the eye and suggest a different role, while meanwhile all sorts of qualified candidates work and study for a chance they'll never get.

"Maybe if you valued me, you wouldn't have treated me with the same respect and attention as the rest of these fauxbeams. You would have asked my opinion and actually listened to it. Not just tried to keep me in my place until I could be useful to you."

Sala's eyes were wide with fury, so much she wasn't even trying to talk. Well, fine, Dime would.

"And what if I had stayed? Ascended to Light's Circle and minded my manners? This would all still be a secret, festering under our skin. We wouldn't be safe from it; it would be building on the inside, growing to the point no one could stop it. *Festering.* The Fo-ror who wish us harm would be festering. Sol's Pillars would be festering. Your boring drills would kill the Fo-ror and restart the Great War and that would not be worth me being here, feeling important, and getting invited to fancy biscuits. Ada-ji is more important than either of us."

"Get out of here." Sala stopped, realizing her error, even as her voice shook with fury. "Out of my office. The guards will escort you to your rooms. I assure you, you'll find them comfortable. Tell us where your family is. Dayn. The children. They'll be treated like distinguished burgesses."

Dime leaned in. "They are distinguished burgesses. And you know what, Sala? The Fo-ror tried to keep me in a room, too. A cage, but still a room, with nice food, access to books or whatever I needed, and even some extraordinarily delightful conversation. If you try and make me stay here, you'll prove my point that we are no different. And I don't suggest you try."

Stepping back, she pointed toward the panel in the floor at the edge of the room. "Esteemed Sala, the Light. I hold you in my regard, and I beg you to consider what I've said. Stop the drilling. Stop it. It's not innocent. It's not science. It's power. I don't understand its aims yet and it sounds like you don't either, but it's power one way or the other. I'm sure of it. If someone is telling you otherwise, I beg you to consider why."

Sala did not react.

Dime lowered her arm, realizing she was still pointing at the floor. "Now. I'm sorry this went bad. I actually am. But I am leaving through that door. You will tell your guards to let me go. They will not stop me, they will not order me, and they will not follow me. Don't even try. Or, I absolutely promise you, you will regret that choice. And most importantly, remember, whether it sounds like it or not right now—I am your ally. If you are on the side of peace, then we are on the same side. I want to help. And when you believe that, you send word."

Sala stood, her eyes furious. "And how am I supposed to send word if I have no idea where you are?"

"The Free Winds. Tell them."

Sala was clearly still livid, but there was a play in her eyes Dime didn't understand. She closed them just a moment, throwing her hands to her temples. "Can you . . . can you stay out of Lodon? At least that?"

"I can't make promises right now, other than to reassure you that I recognize the need to balance voice against order. I will try to be thoughtful. But, Light Sala, I am not hiding again, and I'm not hiding the truth. And if you were *going* to pick me, then that was your mistake. You should have *picked* me."

And with that, Dime flicked her hands, swung open the floor panel, and stepped through it onto the stairs. It was only after the door closed above her that she realized what she'd just done.

Interlude

"**Where** did you get this stuff again? It's great." Mem took a drink of the cloudy beverage, wiggling her fingers against the side of the cup.

"Outforest," Alikago replied.

Sure, like always, he never gave enough information. She'd learned a long time ago one had to be very specific when trying to learn things from fairies, yet here she was still getting single-word answers.

One thing she had to concede was the quality of their ferms. This one tasted clean and herbaceous, and she'd made it perfect by throwing in a rind of some mountain citrus. See, that was the part the Ja-lal had right. Everything needed a good citrus.

"So explain this again," she said, leaning forward against the small, chipped table. Beneath her, the stool gave a creak. "How do you get a ferm without paying for it again? And what incentive is there to even ferment the stuff?"

Alikago kept his face impassive, but his wings twitched a little behind him. She could tell now, that meant he was annoyed.

She had to admit, she'd grown fond of the tall fairy. Enough that she'd been pretty excited he'd agreed to meet up with her on occasion. The dim, dusty ferm tent of the Crossing didn't have the warmth of her village pub—and she imagined a fairy-forest pub would be pretty interesting—but as there was no way for them to meet up at those locations, she made the most of their times relaxing here.

If he weren't a fairy, she'd consider taking it further. But that didn't matter; it was a nice break from shifts at the forge. Also, they were so harmed snooty about their fairy ways, she reminded herself. As she was sure he was about to be again. But, still, she wondered how the whole ferm thing worked without paynotes. She took another sip.

"I can't see how you can ask what incentive there is." He pointed to her. "You're practically glowing as you drink it. So the incentive is: pyrsi like to be happy. So they make ferm."

"Ok, sure. So that's what someone chooses to do with their offbells. How do they get the resources? And who gets to decide who gets some?"

"That's not hard at all. If you have enough resources, like you grow the plants, then you just make it. And you decide. If you need more resources, you petition the Seats. If they decide you get more resources, you do. And then they'll take the extra ferm and distribute it in deliveries."

"Alright. Who decides who gets it?"

"Featherfly, Mem, I just told you. The Seats."

"Well, how do you know they'll be fair?"

She'd pushed that too far. She'd forgotten; these fairies got so defensive when you mentioned their Seats. They closed up like a seedpod every time.

"I'm sorry. Let me ask a different way. Ferm is easy, because pyrsi like it. But what about things pyrsi don't like? No one is going to make nails for fun." So maybe that was not a random point. She *despised* making nails.

Alikago pulled the bottle over and poured himself some more. "Are these serious questions? You think you're trying to encircle me, but I'm most wonderfully still unencumbered. So to answer your question, pyrsi forge nails because they are assigned to do so by the Seats. And it all works. It works great. The Seats ensure everyone has what they need, based on their role. Meanwhile, up in Barrens Reach, your entire system of values is based on paynotes. Want more things? Get more paynotes. The primary flier for our way of life is *values*, and the primary flier for yours is *resources*."

Mem snorted. "I'm glad you believe that. You're so righteous; have you even been to Sol's Reach? Our *resources* allow every pyr to have food and care. And unlike you, it gives them breadth to expand—to try a career, to do something new, to be promoted. They have incentive to do better and so they do. Sounds like our *values* are opportunity and passion. Yours are, what, hoping you can do something with your offbells that you don't dislike as much as your assigned role? And that's your values? No thanks, I'll take ours."

She sipped her drink again, then glancing over at Alikago's, she plucked the citrus rind out of her glass and held it out. With his nod, she tossed it into his cup.

Raising one of his hairy eyebrows—sorry, it was hard not to notice—she waited for him to try the modified drink. Instead, he swirled it under his nose. "Oh, yes, that balances nicely." He tilted some back. "I suppose I owe you some sort of paynote now?"

Somehow, he held his expression while Mem broke out into a laugh.

"What?" he asked, innocently.

"There is nothing in the maintenance of currency that precludes fostering generosity, friend. And too bad your Seats didn't make you an actor," she said. "I'd go to see you."

"You're putting a lot of faith in generosity. Also, you did go to see me. You're right here." He smiled.

Whatever it was in that fairy smile, she would have given him every paynote in her account just to see it again. But she didn't tell him that.

"To Sol," she said, raising her glass. "And . . . Sha."

For once, Alikago didn't have a retort. But their glasses clinked together, and Mem was glad they were here.

Act 2

In Concert

Sala must have sent a webbed command just after Dime left, as the hallways stayed mostly clear on her way out, leaving an eerie silence in the echoey corridors. A few remaining guards and attendants stood still against the walls, staring blankly ahead, neither acknowledging nor attempting to stop her.

About halfway down, finding the situation much more unsettling than previous episodes of commotion and wanting to distract herself from the idea that she'd just casually used fairy valence in front of the Light, she started greeting the guards as she passed. Most kept their gaze ahead, but a few smiled back. This warmed her; it was astonishing how much a smile could mean during a take of trouble.

As she exited the complex and stepped out into the evening breeze, she heard a voice, almost barking out her name. "Dime."

She looked around but didn't see anyone; Sala must have cleared the street as well. It hadn't been a friendly call—Dime felt a shiver in her arms.

"Dime. In the courtyard." She continued down the path and turned into the courtyard. Seeing no one there, she stopped. "Here." The voice rasped from behind a low garden wall, adjacent to a row of cultivated hedges.

As hesitant as she was to step behind a hedge to meet a stranger who wouldn't even show xyr face, there was an urgency to the voice she couldn't ignore. Assuming there wasn't a whole mob in the bushes, she could prevent any one pyr from taking her anywhere, without harm, now. She hoped. And so, first checking again that no one was watching, she hopped over the wall and ducked in between the pruned trunks behind it.

Holy Sol.

"Jaza?" she wheezed, stepping back at the sight of the infamous leader of the Sol's Pillars. There was no question who this was; the fe'pyr was almost a myth among the halls of the complex. The few times she'd appeared in public, she was described just as she appeared now—thick colors over her cheeks, eyes, and mouth. A precise streak of white highlighting her nose. And bright clothing, including a loose orange shirt that hung down over her shoulders, with gaps showcasing the elitist tattoos that ran up her shoulders and neck. Unlike most, she had not tattooed the top of her scalp and face, leaving her unmistakably unique among the Ja-lal.

Most notably, she was alone. No minion to pull Dime aside, no escort to a meeting. Just Jaza, behind a wall. This was indeed strange.

Jaza wrenched her gaze away from Dime's hair-covered scalp, breathing heavily through her nose, like someone winded or trying not to laugh. "How are things?" Jaza casually tipped her head, as though they were good friends, but there was an anger in her eyes that was baked in. Old. Dime knew in that moment she would need to be very careful.

"It's been better," she answered, with a forced smile. "So, uh, since we're here, maybe ask your mobs to back off my children?" They were out of the city, but she'd rather leave that unclear to Jaza, and it wasn't as if they could be asked to stay out forever.

"Your children won't be safe when the Fo-ror invade Sol's Reach." Jaza's mouth twisted into a snarl, then faded back again. "Besides, they do what they want."

"No," Dime said, shaking her head. "No. They take cues from you."

"Sometimes," Jaza said. "All I do is encourage pyrsi to say what they were already thinking. Don't see how that's my fault."

"Really? I do." Dime wasn't interested in trading barbs; she had better things to do. "Why'd you follow me? Why'd you call me back here? We're talking in the bushes, you know. Not too impressive for a supremacist?"

Jaza broke into a laugh. "True, true. Fine, then, no chit chat. I was wondering what your thoughts were on current events."

That I'm tired of being pummeled by them?

Alright, Dime had come back to Lodon to talk, and if Jaza was a willing ear, she'd try her. "I think . . . that for whatever reasons, consciousness about Ja-lal and Fo-ror contact has now spread into open dialogue. Pyrsi on both sides will continue to see each other; it's not going away. Pyrsi will grow bolder also. They will start to take risks, and venture over the cliff on their own. Some will see what they want, and others will see normal pyrsi, a lot like themselves. I think it's imperative that any pyr with a voice—and you most definitely qualify—use that voice to promote calm, listening, and understanding. To encourage pyrsi to get together, to—"

"I see I wasted my time finding you," Jaza interrupted, her voice thinning. "I thought you'd be better than some naïve little Circles mouthpiece. I thought you'd have learned by now *some idea* of what the Fo-ror are capable of." Her eyes narrowed.

The irony of that. Dime did have some idea. More than most. She just wasn't going to tell this divider her own story, give her any more fuel to light her torch. "Valence is just a tool. They have no reason to use it for harm, not if we work together. How could we not owe it to ourselves to give them that chance?"

Jaza rolled her eyes, disgust darkening them.

Dime wondered whether the rumors of her own valence would leak. She felt it unlikely Sala would tell anyone, wanting any controversy to recede, not be incited. And so far, it seemed those who had seen her make the rift outside the city had attributed it to some ambiguous "witchcraft" rather than specifically fairy valence. But someone would figure that out eventually; the uncertainty of when and how had circled in Dime's mind, a constant worry.

Maybe, she considered, she should just show Jaza her valence now. Be out with it. Let her know she wasn't someone to be played with. Yet it was hard, standing here behind a hedge, to see where all the paths would lead. What the impact of her choices would be. And she didn't like the idea of waving around an ability. She stared back at the pyr, contemplating her options.

"I see you're of no use to me," Jaza finally said, stepping back and surveying her up and down. "And that hair is disgusting. *Shave it*," she hissed.

"Why, do I look like a fairy? Does that bother you?" Dime raised her eyebrows. Ok, at least she'd kept those shaven.

Dime didn't expect the growl that came from Jaza's mouth and with the way she raised her hands, Dime had no idea what she might do. For the first time in her life, she had the sensation of someone wanting to strike her. Fear coursed upward and downward, sending a dizzying shiver through her nose and her fingertips. She stumbled backward, just to run into something solid behind her.

As Dime spun around, Jaza's growl turned into a full-throated laugh.

"Oh, look! You've been *rescued!*"

Dime looked up and found herself face-to-face with none other than Rock. *Harm it!*

"Oh, I was just in the area," Rock chimed.

Familiar with Rock's demeanor, Dime saw that she was struggling to regain her composure. She always overcompensated when she was thrown off, which actually wasn't often. But still, Rock had followed her here like she was a ch'pyr!

"Agent Rock, my great pleasure to finally meet you! Love your lip color! What shade is it? I may have to try it." Jaza tapped her own orange lips. "I've heard Dime here loves blue."

"Oh, I actually do," Dime said, jumping in. She wasn't going to let Jaza get away with that.

Jaza glanced at her crosswise. "Well, the Circles will be interested by your close affiliation, won't they?"

Dime had an answer for that too, but Rock stepped around her.

"I don't get threatened," she said. "You tell anyone whatever you want. It'll come out of the same drainpipe as the rest of your sludge. Go ahead—go in and talk to the IC. I'm sure they'd love to talk to you." Rock flicked her nose up. "And be sure to tell them I said hi. Dime. Let's get out of here. I don't like chatting with supremacists, especially ones who hide in the trees."

Maybe her fairy sensibilities were growing, but it seemed sort of silly to hear Rock refer to a line of pointy shrubs as trees. Not relevant though; she agreed with Rock. "Yeah, I was just leaving myself. But nice of you to pop in?"

Realizing the absurdity of their situation, both fe'pyrsi broke into laughter. Any annoyance Dime had at Rock dissipated and she beamed at her friend's sincere smile. Jaza, however, wasn't seeing the joke.

"Keep laughing," she spat. "Keep laughing." She turned right to Dime. "The fairies *will pay* for what they've done." She glanced over at Rock, hesitating, then turned back. "And if you choose to side with them, so will you."

Enough of this. This pyr had no interest in dialogue. "Rock, you're right," she sighed, annoyed that her voice shook a little. Well, this pyr had done more than disrupt her life. And she had the nerve to pull her back here, what, to taunt her? "Let's go."

Jaza made no move to stop them as the two stepped back out onto the walkway.

"Come on, let's get out of sight," Rock whispered. "I mean, a different place out of sight. Follow me." Together, they ran, not stopping until they'd dropped past the main road and wound around a long series of alleyways. Rock ducked back through a door, and into an empty room, unfurnished, like for storage or sheltering a toothcar. Light streamed into the dark space through high, narrow windows. Relaxing, Dime sat back onto the floor, immediately regretting the decision, as it was filthy.

"I thought your hideaway would be cleaner?"

Rock was still standing, light from the window spotlighting the side of her face. "Not my hideaway. Give me more credit. Just know of it and wanted to get you out of sight. Oh, and it's good to see you?"

"It's good to see you too." It came off terse, but Dime was still feeling terse, after the Light, and then Jaza. Harm, the leader of Sol's Pillars! But at least Rock was an ally. No, a friend. Dime wasn't going to risk an argument. She took a breath, trying to just be glad to see her.

"Look, you're going to be mad at me," Rock said.

"I'm already mad at you; just tell me what's next." *Whoops. That slipped out.* Hopefully she'd take it as a joke. I mean, she wasn't serious. She'd let it go.

"Sure. Well, I've been thinking about what you said so I stopped by to talk to Olok, and—"

"I told you not to bother her!" Dime sprung back to her feet. Olok was a medic who they'd decided was likely another of Neimano's victims. Unlike the others, Dime had reason to believe Olok was aware of her biology. So there was no reason to bother her, when she'd clearly just been trying to live a normal life, from what Dime knew. Why had Rock barged in on the pyr? They'd discussed this. Rock couldn't presume to know what learning their history had been like. It wasn't her lane. "You said we were a team," she said instead.

"Right. A team. Not you ordering me around."

Dime was so annoyed, she just let her keep talking.

"So you were right, anyway. I'm admitting it to you. She does know, and she doesn't want anyone else to know, and she doesn't want anything to do with you, or bringing pyrsi back together, or any of it. Says she's doing important psychological research that's helping real pyrsi, and it wouldn't be right to disrupt it."

"I told you not to bother her."

"Yes, you mentioned it. And here I'm being honest with you. I told you I talked to her. I told you, you were essentially right. Olok told me to flick off. Maybe let's just be out with it—are you telling me the same thing?"

Sol. Rock was so difficult. Dime hadn't said a word about separating. Whatever that even meant. No, she knew what it meant. They'd made a promise to work together to prevent a war. She couldn't lose Rock. Though, her friend was even older than she was; Dime shouldn't have to coddle her. "No. I'm not telling you any such thing." Despite her efforts to hold her temper back, she figured she could get away with one last comment. "But you knew I didn't want you to talk to her. You did it anyway. Now you hold it over me like I'm endangering our team."

"Team," Rock repeated. "Team. Maybe there's something you need to know, D. I'm no one's sidekick. So you're a fairy. Good. And I'm not. Unless you've become a fairy supremacist to balance out your brute pal back there, that makes us equals."

"What the kill, Rock?" That was way too far. "What do you think Jaza and I were up to back there? Are—"

The question *Are you jealous?* hung out in the air like little words written of clouds and Dime was certain Rock could see them.

Rock drew in a breath. "I'm sorry. None of this is about that or anything like it. I've never seen Jaza up close before. There was a poison in her, like I could see her reaching out to harm you. It set me off. I'm sorry."

Dime tried to think what to say. She had felt the same thing, that Jaza would actually have used the Violence. That to her it wasn't forbidden. If she had it to do over again, she never would have jumped behind that wall.

Rock went on. "And I shouldn't have talked to Olok. I knew that, and I did it anyway. I had . . . reasons, but they don't stand up so I'm not getting into them. So I'm sorry. I'm sorry about everything except one thing. You promised to be a team. Don't boss me around."

Just then, the bells broke out across the city, and though muted within the thick stone walls, it was too loud to continue. Dime glanced around, waiting until the final echoes subsided.

"That's fair," she finally answered. She was going to ask what Rock thought about Jaza, but it was sort of obvious from her last words. Clearly neither of them saw her as someone who was going to turn, or help, or any such thing. That's fine. They'd work around her.

"If you want out of the deal . . ."

"I don't."

"Ok."

The silence was awkward. Were they supposed to hug? Dime . . . couldn't.

"D. I'm on your side."

"I know, Rock. That means a lot. And, hey, I've been thinking a lot. Just about that."

The room was dim, but she could see Rock raise her eyebrows.

"I mean, not about you, I mean, yes about you, but—what I'm trying to say is I've thought a lot about the idea of being alone. Alone in this. Sala was right about something. We've been running around, you, me, Dayn, Ador. That's got to stop. We need more pyrsi. It's time to go open. It's time to speak up."

Rock nodded. "I agree with you, if you're asking."

Dime ignored the barb, though she silently reminded herself to make sure she consulted with Rock. After all, she really did trust her insights. And as much as it had shocked and annoyed her that she'd burst in to take Dime's side with Jaza back there, it was comforting. She hoped Jaza was intimidated, seeing who she was up against. *She should be.*

"I'd like your opinion on this, then." She'd been intending to return to the hut by dark, as she hadn't packed for an extended stay. But with Rock here, maybe they were best to start putting things in motion. Dayn would understand; it would take more than a few bells before he worried. "I'm thinking about going back to talk to Volana, one of the fairies who met us at the den. I'd like to see if she's made any inroads on speaking to the Foundry, and I can let her know what

I'm thinking, too. We clearly have a lot of work to do here, but if we can get her moving there, we'll be running the cars on both sides of the road. Would be good to know where it all stands."

"Makes sense." Rock's voice twinged a little. Dime remembered she'd avoided meeting with the fairies last time. She figured it was best to just ask.

"You seem nervous meeting with her." Anyway, that was as close to asking as she'd take it.

Rock sighed. "Yeah, it's nothing weird. I've just been working these cycles to understand the fairies; to really just hang out with one feels . . . odd. Yeah, I know there's you, but you're D. And I know I carved birds for half the pyrsi of norside Pito, but also different. When I'm in a cage, I'm an agent. Ja-lal in distress. It's not the same as . . . real life."

Dime wasn't totally sure she understood, but she was glad Rock would be going with her.

"Where are the others?" Rock scratched behind her ear.

"Which others?" *Ador, maybe?*

"Your spouse? Children?"

"Oh, they're hidden." She was perfectly comfortable telling her where, but without knowing for sure if anyone could be listening, she kept that out. She knew Rock would get that.

"Dayn must not like that."

What? Hmm. "Anyway, there's one more thing, and it's . . . even weirder."

"Of course it is."

"I also owe the newts twice now, so if we're going that way, I think we should check on them as well. If you're willing."

"Always willing, D."

Relieved they'd worked things out for the stride, Dime swept a slight wind across her backside, brushing off loose dirt from the floor. Which reminded her.

"Well, there's one more thing. We'll be, uh, flying."

Rock grinned. "I'd expect no less."

While making their way back to her chair, Dime thought about how best to fly the both of them. Not wanting to leave the chair here and knowing how intense moving disconnected objects had been over a long distance, there seemed an obvious easiest choice. But, would she?

She waited until they stood in front of the wooden chair. "So this is awkward." Dime grimaced at Rock's teasing expression. "Anyway. The easiest way to do this is for you to sit on my, er, lap. Now, we don't have to," she clarified. "I have other ideas."

Rock was chortling. "What are the other ideas?"

"So I thought maybe I could raise a stick. And each of us could hold onto the stick. We'd have to cling to it, well, anyway, I don't want to leave my chair here. So then I thought, well we can each perch on one arm of the chair, and—"

"D. We're Gamhs. Let's just go the one-chair way. And next time you have your tools, make me a sidecar."

She snapped her head around to see Rock almost crying with laughter.

"Sol, Rock," she muttered.

They were both laughing by the time Dime kept poking the thinner pyr, telling her to stop wriggling as they tried to situate themselves. Yet, with all the practice she'd now had, and her desire to get out of this arrangement as soon as possible, it was no effort to rise together into the air. They hovered over the small garden, Dime figuring out the shortest way to get out of view.

"That way," she decided, pointing. "Only need to pass a few towers before we'll reach the wall."

"What if pyrsi are looking out of their windows?" Rock gasped through her chuckles.

"They'll have a great story that they'll be too nervous to tell pyrsi. Now, let's go."

Together, they zipped off, out of the city and across Sol's Reach. Dime tried to imagine Rock's expression as she saw the towers, the wall, and the outcity corridor from above. And after a couple breaks to stretch as well as try again to stay their laughter, Dime saw the Great Cliff dropping off before them, casting an almost endless shadow over the green treetops in the waning light. Dime landed near its top.

"Cold . . . chair?" Rock inquired. "Scenic moment?"

"No, just need to look at this map." If she weren't worried about losing the daylight, she *would* have stayed longer for the view. Instead, she unfolded a sheet of paper Volana had given her, trying to memorize the details before tucking it back into a pocket. Gladly, it was clear enough to follow, with the aid of the landmarks, such as the arched entrance to the Seats' complex and the broad area labeled *commons* to guide her.

Dime had to concentrate, both to spot each marker, and also to weave through the trees—which was profoundly more complicated than zooming over the plains, especially now in the dimming light.

Hoping they were near their destination, she landed one more time, trying to avoid being seen so they could consult the map again. It did look like they were close; she'd just passed that tri-forked path. Sol, she thought that flight would never end.

She supposed this was a residential area, with the normal browns, greens, and rustles of the forest but small paths and gardens, and that perfect mix of forest musk striped by the breeze. It was hard not to feel a little jealous of the pyrsi who lived here, but then, she did love city life.

Gathering herself, she read the number that Volana had marked. She didn't know where to find it on the structures. Or the trees? Were there signs? Dime knew where to look on a building, but not on a tree.

Really not wanting to knock at the wrong home, despite the fact that she wouldn't know how to knock at a curtain anyway, Dime called up into the branches. "Volana?" She waited, hoping Volana had heard her; she didn't want to make a scene.

It was Uchitar who lowered to the ground, his gray robes fluttering as his wings moved in firm, uneven motion. Dime watched in fascination as a patch of three-leaf rippled at his approach, yet Uchitar didn't notice, as though descending from a tree was as ordinary as breathing. His clothes had been cleaned and repaired, and he had more . . . life to his face than she remembered. Despite clear surprise in his expression, he quickly offered a broad smile and a wave of his fingers.

Dime rushed forward, and they clasped hands. "Uchitar! So good to see you again." She turned around. "This is my friend, Fe'Rock."

"Rock, like the . . . rock?" Uchitar winced, but Rock took it in stride.

"Name's actually Fe'Rika. Don't tell. Pyrsi like D call me Rock because I'm strong like rock." She flexed her biceps, whose ripples, impressively, could be seen even through her thin top.

Dime laughed. Rock was well aware of the silliness of her fictitious background, but it cheered her to see the pyr puffing this way to the smiling fairy. But, Dime wanted to get out of sight. "Uchitar. If you fly to the right structure, we'll follow. Just, er, trust me."

Uchitar looked troubled, but apparently not about Dime's ability to follow. "Structure? You mean her home?"

"Sure, yes, her home." Sometimes the terms were the same and sometimes they were different. Dime never knew.

"Follow me, then." Uchitar flapped up into the trees. Without wanting to make a big deal of it, Dime got in the chair and Rock followed, with a brief awkward glance before she sat back down on Dime's lap. Together, they lifted upward.

Dime was fairly proud of how easily she set the chair onto the planked walkway, with only one wobble and one loud *thunk*. Rock hopped right off.

They looked around; it would be hard not to amongst the serenity of the long shadows peeking through the swaying branches, which rustled like a calming whisper. Dime heard the clinking of a small chime, but didn't see where it hung. The exterior of the home was lined with vertical boards, and a thatched roof rested overhead, sheltering the walkway as well.

"This way." Uchitar pointed toward a curtain, hanging on the curved wall.

"You walk in through the curtains. I don't think they have doors," Dime whispered to Rock.

"I'm the one in Dawn's Circle," Rock whispered back. "I know. But . . . I don't have tree shoes."

Tree shoes? Oh, yes, the thin slippers Ella had made for her were still tucked in a side pocket of her bag, though they must be crushed flat by now. As Rock removed her boots, she apologized to Uchitar for her dirty socks. Dime thought she heard Uchitar make a joke about Volana and vomit and socks, and decided she didn't really want to hear the rest.

Dime set her boots next to Rock's, and wriggled her feet into the flattened slippers, with almost no sole to them. She wasn't sure how these were much more polite than socks. She took one last look around outside, glad to see no signs anyone had noticed their arrival. Sol was quickly setting; she was grateful they'd made it here first.

She watched the way that Uchitar and Rock entered the home and tried to emulate it. Which really wasn't hard, it was just pushing the curtain aside and stepping through. Well, Rock pushed it aside. Uchitar sort of powered in and let the curtain swing where it would.

"Volana's not here now. She's been letting me stay." He turned to Rock. "I've been a tzetz addict. Our relationship is as friends."

"Ours too!" Rock added, pointing to Dime, and Dime pretended not to hear. "But I'm sorry to hear about the tzetz. Tough road. I hope you can keep to your path here."

"*Mmm.*" He glanced around, his hands clasped together. He seemed unable to answer.

Rock scanned the room. "So, Volana is on shift?"

Uchitar breathed in. "Probably not anymore. She left a while ago. She's been seeing someone. Ma'Eytanii. He sounds really nice." Dime noticed there wasn't any concern in Uchitar's voice; if anything, he sounded happy that Volana had found a companion. She hadn't suspected any romance between her friends, but she had no idea if Uchitar had any family or arrangements himself.

Rock was still gazing off at the wall.

"Oh, that's fun," Dime said, thinking someone should answer. "This is her home? And no one else lives here?" She wasn't sure whether that was normal for a tree home, but Uchitar seemed to understand her question. And it wasn't a large place—it reminded her of a starter home midcity. A living space opened into a compact kitchen area, separated by a countertop. To the other side, a wall and curtains separated what was likely a sleeping room.

"Yes, just Volana, until the ba'pyr is born. She's got me staying on the cushions—" He pointed to a couple of large pillows in what looked like it had been a reading nook, or maybe a small social area, before Uchitar took it over. "It's unusual to live alone in the city, but Volana is particular about company, and somehow she talked home allocation into a nice place. She can be persuasive." He grinned. "Honestly, it's driving her to wingtwitch that I'm here."

He looked over at Rock. "She takes care of junkies on her offshifts. She's trying to keep me away from it for a while. Kind of embarrassing, but that's where we are."

Rock curled in her fingers. It was a gesture of encouragement; hopefully here as well. "Keep with it then. And some advice? Don't repeat their slurs. That's two now."

"It gets in your head," he said, a tremble to the words. "Hey, though, are you hungry? Thirsty? There's a common bath outside. Volana's got nice filtered water here. And I found her some soft-fruits." He pointed to a basket of blushed, mushy-looking fruit. "I went a little far with it, so there's plenty to share."

Dime remembered Ella talking about Suzannelina's complaints

regarding food rations. But it felt too soon to ask about something like that.

"Sure, that would be nice," Rock walked over and picked up one of the fruits, licking the juice that ran over her fingers. "Ripe ones! Mmm," she followed. "Haven't had anything this good since the dead caves."

"You were in the dead caves?" Uchitar sat back on a low stool, his knees jutting up awkwardly under his robe. Dime noticed he was wringing his hands, much like before.

"Sure was! Luckily, Dime here came and rescued me."

Dime knew better than to argue with that.

"It's a running joke at the creek," Uchitar said. "You want good food, you spend a little time in the caves. Some of the tougher-luck pyrsi do it to recharge. I never did— So anyway, it's a loophole, I guess. Same kitchens serve the Seats as serve the prison. The Seats are so used to good food, they don't know the extent to which they've upgraded any prisoners used to standard rations."

Realizing it might be rude not to, Dime went over and took one of the fruits from the dark wooden bowl. She couldn't help but laugh at Rock, who was holding a few large, slippery pits in her hand, wriggling her sticky fingers, as if she were going to touch Dime with them.

Uchitar showed them how to turn on a faucet, and the running water made an interesting noise that Dime found pleasant. If she had wings, she would have hopped outside to see whether there was metal plumbing here, or an exterior collection system. It seemed too soon to ask; she didn't want to give the impression of evaluating their lives. Even if it was pure curiosity.

Remembering that Uchitar had been living on the floor cushions, she instead chose a padded wicker bench to the other side of the curtain.

"Her home is beautiful," she offered, gazing around at the simple yet lovely dwelling. Dried herbs and flowers were bundled near the entrance, almost as if creating a ward. Cheerful embroidery hung from brightly dyed strings, and several books stood together over a painted stand. Only Uchitar's corner looked a little disheveled. And it wasn't as if he were being a rude guest. It was all situated well enough. But it stood in contrast to the simple style with which Volana had arranged the rest.

As the room grew dark, Uchitar charged the glowstones with a touch. And after a while, Volana arrived, full of greetings and rushing to see what else the visitors needed.

Seeing Dime and Rock continue to yawn, she asked again and again if they couldn't spare time to rest before they talked, and Dime finally relented. Volana showed them into her bedroom and wouldn't hear any protests about taking her space. "I'll rest when you leave. I have several spans before I need to go out. It's fine."

Fortunately, Volana had a folding, if rickety, wood ramp that she lowered with a crank and ropes. She said it was for when her mothers came to visit, but she used it for deliveries as well. Glad the walkway didn't bounce too much and grateful she didn't have to help Rock fly, they were able to walk down and find the bath. And Dime was relieved that no one, for now, asked about the strange-looking chair parked on the walkway.

Thinking again how the rich forest was the setting of ordinary life here, Dime stood alone a take, listening to the sounds of the forest—both rhythmic and chaotic—and of the fairy dwellings, nestled above. Through the trees, she thought she heard the strain of a violin. No, lower, like in baritone.

She'd lost track of how long it had been since she'd slept, but she was as tired as if it'd been even longer. Not even Rock's jagged snoring kept Dime awake once she laid down her head.

Of course Rock awoke first. Dime could hear her in the main room, telling stories in an animated tone. Trying to make herself half as chipper, Dime dragged back down the ramp and washed up. Before climbing up, she gazed around at the trees again, rustling in the night. Volana's home was much lower to the ground than most others she'd seen, and especially compared to the dwellings that rose all the way into the canopy near the city's center.

She supposed Volana had requested one at this level if her mothers required a ramp. Yet, looking at other structures in the surrounding trees, none rose too high. It seemed perhaps the further away from the city . . . or, she supposed, the complex, one went, the lower xyr home would be. It must be easier to build closer to the ground, so it made sense.

This was somewhat like Lodon, in that the high structures dwindled to low ones closer to the wall, but with one notable difference. Here, while she'd seen some evidence of multi-layer structures, they were generally staggered, with more space separating each. And Uchitar had indicated pyrsi lived more to a home. Certainly, building a structure into a tree was much different than building structures to rest on each other. There was still so much she didn't know.

She put on a smile as she entered the main room, amused to find Uchitar engaged in lively story trade with Rock. He was more relaxed than she'd seen him, which was nice. Volana sat at her counter, sipping something warm from a cup.

Seeing Dime, she pointed to a waiting plate and cup, thin steam rising from the cup. "I hope you don't mind; Rock told me what you like and don't like." Volana didn't appear to mean anything by it other than polite precautions against dietary issues, but either way, Dime didn't bother to look Rock's direction. She knew the squint she'd have on her face, and she didn't feel like seeing it.

"So I'm here for a couple of reasons. Or a few," Dime offered, sipping what turned out to be a really subtle tea. "First, I wanted to see you. With everything that's going on, I sometimes . . . get lost in a world that's expanded to both sides of the cliff." Having friends on both of those sides helped ground her to it, but she didn't quite know how to say that part.

No one else seemed to know how to respond either, so Dime continued. "And I wanted to see if you'd had any reaction from the Foundry. Not to pry," she clarified. "I've just really understood lately how important that it is not just to work together, but to bring others in with us. It's the only way to move forward."

She set down the tea, looking longingly at the toast on her plate. But she wanted to finish the thought first. "So I'm curious how that went. I suppose, whatever this movement is, I view you as leading it on this side."

Rock nodded, but otherwise the room might has well have been frozen in a painting. Feeling awkward, Dime went on. "Also, I wanted to talk to you about the newts. I thought, as you're addressing things, you could learn more about them. You probably know they're kept out of the forest by a diamond-dusted net. This also keeps them from their long-time home, Home Sha. It's a large lake to the sur."

"I have heard of Newt Lake," Volana said, discomfort on her face. "But I didn't know . . . well, please continue."

Dime was unable to hide her grimace at the new term for the lake. "It's their home. The lake provides them fresh water, as they don't have raincatchers or plumbing. Without the lake, they are suffering on long beaches, barely protected from the wind and drinking the harsh Sha water. And, before you ask, yes, I've tried drinking it. I couldn't even keep it in my mouth. No one should have to live that way, but it's worse knowing their level of sentience. The newts aren't anything like how they're described." Her own experience was in Sol's Reach, but by Ferala's words, they weren't thought of better here. "They're intelligent, not in the way that we are, but enough that they are suffering greatly in their current state."

"Newts." Volana spun a stirrer, seeming distant and distracted. "I did not expect you to come here to talk about newts." She laid the stick down. "I trust you. And I will ask more about this. And let you know." Volana stared off across the counter.

Dime had never been great at social skills. She'd gone through the reasons why she was here, and each seemed to evoke a silence more poignant than the last. Giving up, she spun her fork into some glistening green threads.

"I did talk to the Foundry," Volana finally offered, while Dime was crunching through a piece of toast. "It caused a lot of conversation, more than I would ever have expected. Pyrsi here are . . . interested in the Ja-lal. And perhaps the complement is true where you live."

Rock didn't say anything about this, but Dime noticed she whispered a few words to Uchitar then came over to join them.

"It was a mixed response," Volana continued. "At first I felt like the others were unsure. I didn't know if it was because I was bold enough to say it, or because pyrsi were still thinking about how to respond. Some spoke of caution during the meeting. Yet I know what caution meant, at least to them. Some were loudly against my ideas. They reiterated the same lines I've grown up hearing. The Violence. The brutes. The same. But . . . these were not the worst. I am used to them."

She grimaced. "Some talked to me afterward. They thanked me. Said I was on a good flypath. They said they agreed and said it was time for me to hand these discussions over to the leadership." She turned sharply toward Dime. "A few turns ago, I would have. But you had me thinking. Why can't I be a part of this?"

Dime nodded. She knew that Volana was considered low class by the Fo-ror, an unchangeable circumstance in their minds. She didn't expect Rock to address the idea openly.

"Volana?" Rock waited for Volana to turn her way. "I've studied the Fo-ror for cycles and I wanted to see if I got something right. I think the reason Ja-lal have a hard time understanding Fo-ror class is that we apply our own prejudices to it." Dime had no idea what she meant by that.

"The Ja-lal view high-class as better and low-class as worse, and they strive to increase their standing. The Fo-ror are more rigid in their characterization, but to most pyrsi just living their lives, they accept class as an immovable fact. And in that acceptance, there is less shame to it. Someone is low class because they are low class. There is less negativity associated with that. It's only when someone tries to act outside of their class that others bristle. How . . . accurate is that?"

Volana thought what seemed to be a very long time. This was something else Dime had realized she'd need to adjust to. Fo-ror took much longer to form a response; Dime tended to get impatient at the delay. But their answers were no less valid for the wait; usually, they were more reasoned. So Dime kept quiet.

"Yes," Volana finally answered. "I've never heard it discussed in those terms, so it is odd to try and think that way. Think like a Ja-lal," she said, rounding the word *Ja-lal* as if it were still new. "That will help me, I think, dealing with the Foundry. To think, not, 'this is the way things are' but 'this is the way we think.' Those are different; thank you."

"Then you're not letting them take you out of it?" Dime was glad to hear that.

Volana huffed. "Of course not!" She mock-raised her chin, as her wings angled behind her. "Look at me. Ja-lal in my home! No, I am carrying this delivery. If others want in, they can grab the blanket too." She grinned, as Uchitar beamed from the background.

"But,"—her smile disappeared—"Ador was right about the temperature changing." Dime didn't think she meant that literally. "The Risers, the group that whispers about claiming Sol's Reach, they are becoming more aggressive. More meetings. Fewer whispers. More communication with others."

"Like Sol's Pillars," Dime offered.

"I don't know enough about Sol's Pillars to say," Volana said with a shrug. "Oh! But there is something important I need to tell you! Sha's waves—I got distracted by the meal!" She pointed to her cutting board.

Dime could certainly see why; the crispy bread spread with

salted bulb cream and a smear of the softfruit was one of the most elegant things she'd had in a while. For some reason, she thought back to Nafat and his fancy array of finger food. She thought he'd love this more. But—what was Volana's news?

"The discussions have become so disruptive, with pyrsi even not showing for shift out of fear of impending danger, that the High Seat will be speaking at commons! Tonight, at centernight."

Dime turned over to Rock, who was already looking her way, a sparkle in her eye. She almost laughed; so Rock would definitely be there. Dime supposed she would stay as well. "We'd like to go," she said. "Rock and I."

"Ja-lal? In the audience of the High Seat?" Uchitar's voice rang through.

"I've been in his audience before," Dime said, not expecting that kind of dismissal from her friend.

"No," Uchitar walked closer. "I don't mean as in prejudice. I mean, wouldn't that be disruptive? Maybe pyrsi need to hear from the High Seat. Seeing you there could, well, a lot of things could happen. It worries me."

Dime felt embarrassed for having misunderstood him. She'd become so accustomed to thinking of the Ja-lal and Fo-ror as coinhabitants, she'd almost forgotten the underlying premise: that they weren't. "It'll be dark," she offered.

"They can sit in the branches," Volana added. "We'll just be shapes up there. If we all sit together, our wings will create the right backdrop, and I don't think anyone will parse the rest of it out. As long as we don't draw attention."

"We'll have to figure how to get them into the trees." Uchitar tapped his chin. "Do we trust any lifters?"

Dime made a decision. "There's something I need to tell you. I ask that it doesn't leave this room." Unlike her first few times revealing her secret, it was almost becoming old news to her. Boring. Of course she was biologically Fo-ror. And so she told them. "There's a history behind it, and I hope you don't mind if I keep that held close a little longer." Frankly, she wasn't sure if knowing Neimano's role would put her friends at any risk.

Volana nodded solemnly. Though, her reaction would be different if Dime had told her that her wings had been removed without consent, not that she was born that way or there had been a medical issue. Uchitar didn't seem surprised, but maybe he'd already surmised it.

"So I don't have wings, but I do have valence. I've learned to use it. And,"—she reminded herself she'd already decided to trust her friends—"this." She pulled the diamond out from her collar. "It packs some zing."

"May I see it?" Volana asked. The fairy, much taller than Dime, leaned forward and cradled the stone in her hand. When she stepped back, there were tears in her eyes. "I've never seen one before," she said.

All Dime could see in her mind were caves and caves of the stone, making hers, in a different context, unremarkable. But it was not unremarkable, and, she reminded herself, it held cycles and cycles of her own energy. And Volana had never even seen one.

Dime glanced over at the ma'pyr. "Uchitar, mind if I straighten up your sleeping area?"

"What? Sure?" Uchitar tilted his head, clearly unsure where she was going with the request.

Dime twisted over and swung her hand around. All the cushions spun back, leaning themselves into neat rows against the wall. She swept the dirt from the floor under them and pushed it out of the window. She reached into the herbs by the door, pinched away just a bit of their essence, and perfumed the air, leaving a lingering scent of wildflowers.

She turned to see Volana's reaction, and was surprised to see almost no expression at all.

"Don't worry, Volana, *I'm* still the real deal," Rock joked. "Some rogue agent, hanging out with a group of fairies." She leaned back, but then forgetting the chairs didn't have backs, tumbled backward.

Dime rushed a cushion of air under her, and Rock levitated a moment before setting gently to the ground.

"I am what I am," Dime said. "But I needed you to know."

"That's Second Seat Ji'Layanie," Volana whispered, pointing down to the tall ji'pyr standing next to Ferala. "It's good to see ve's here as well. They are both individually revered, but speaking together shows unity and respect."

"Neimano not so much?" Dime offered.

Volana didn't answer; Dime continued to forget how uncomfortable talking about the Seats in anything but reverent terms made the Fo-ror. She gazed down at both Seats, standing on an illuminated circular stage, surrounded by tall trees, each pruned back to allow viewing space from above, as well as from those seated on the ground cover below, lined with low benches.

Ferala looked as she'd seen him before. Dark robes, and white braids swaying together in three gathered groups, for she could now see the one that hung between his wings. Metallic, silver threads woven through his hair caught the light of the glowstones, as did his diamond-laden fingers. His face showed no expression, other than a slow scan of the crowd and the trees. Dime wondered if he was looking for her.

Beside him, Second Seat Layanie stood, with hair tinted a light shade of blue and wearing a gathered, flowing robe—if a Ja-lal had worn it, Dime would have called it a gown—laced with ribbon flowers. Vis was an intriguing combination of lightness and gravity; Layanie did not look like someone to try and subvert. Dime wondered what vis thoughts were on ruling, stuck between the tension of High Seat Ferala and Third Seat Neimano.

Actually, Dime had a sudden impression ve handled it just fine.

"My hood itches," Rock complained on her other side, jarring her from her thoughts. In Rock's shuffling to adjust the fabric, she bumped Dime's arm. Dime almost scooted further down, but Volana was right there.

"*Hmm?* Oh. See, I told you. You need hair." The hoods, which they'd fashioned from one of Volana's fabric scraps, were a bit scratchy, but it was also true that Dime's soft layer of hair helped. "It's great," she said, tapping the top of her hood.

"No chance."

"Uchitar, ok down there?" The ma'pyr was on Rock's other side, fidgeting as though aggravated. He gave her a smile, which Dime returned. Seeming to take Dime's cue, since shouting down the branch didn't really fit their intent to stay low-key, Rock angled to face Uchitar, talking to him while they sat and waited. Volana was still absorbed in the surroundings, so Dime turned her attention back to the stage.

It seemed the leaders were waiting for more pyrsi to gather; a dwindling stream of Fo-ror flew in, looking for spots to sit. The watching Seats looked surprised, as if gatherings weren't usually this well-attended. Noting their scans, Dime kept her face shielded in the shadows under her hood. She'd sworn not to hide, but she could rationalize that remaining inconspicuous at someone else's event was not at all the same thing.

Then she heard a murmuring among the crowd, growing rapidly from a tiny buzz to a clamor—a pointing of fingers toward one of the rows of benches. There, a pyr sat, wearing pants, leaning on a walking stick, and with tattoos of leaves covering her dark skin. *Ella!*

Ferala and Layanie were staring Ella's way with stunned expressions. Layanie held up a hand, indicating for the audience to quiet. They did.

"State your business." There was no question to whom Layanie spoke.

Ella's voice did not falter, and Dime clutched Rock, suddenly feeling dizzy. "I am Ella, spouse of Suzannelina of the village of Noruh, long since passed to memory. I am concerned regarding the unrest spreading in both lands, so I traveled here to see for myself. If I am yet unwelcome, I will take my leave."

It looked as though Layanie was about to take her up on the offer, but Ferala stepped forward. "Ella. It is a rare event to have a Ja-lal amongst us, but I recognize you have a unique connection to our kind. Our pots are yours to share." He bowed.

A low rustle sped through the crowd, as if pyrsi were compelled to react to this development, but still knew they could not interrupt or subvert their High Seat. Dime glanced around, wondering if Neimano was there. She half expected him to leap from the shadows. Definitely wearing a cape.

But, she thought, perhaps he was secluded in the trees, as Dime and Rock were. If he were, she had a feeling that he would not reveal himself without great cause. She pulled her hood forward.

Ferala used some sort of trick, well not a trick but valence, to amplify his voice on the wind. As he could clearly no longer just say what he had intended to, he seemed now to only want to get on with it, before the unrest escalated. Dime wondered whether pyrsi would be allowed to speak of this afterward, of Ella's unexpected presence. *There's no way they can stop them.* She supposed Ferala knew that.

Only then did Dime notice that Tikinal was there also, seated on a stool to one side of the stage. As he was used to blending in among the Seats, Dime hadn't even noticed him. Which was not trivial, given the attractive nature of the quiet clerk. She felt elated to see him again, and wished they could talk. Silently she whispered a hello into the air and sent it his way. She almost thought he turned.

Ferala didn't do much of the talking. If he'd meant to, Ella's presence seemed to distract him. Or maybe he knew he'd pushed something sensitive with Layanie by inviting the Ja-lal to stay. Layanie was not deterred by any of it; ve stood and addressed the rumors of Ja-lal in Pito. Which were much harder to wave past with Ella sitting right there.

Slowly Dime understood why Ella was here. She almost burst

off her own hood and slid to the ground, but then she remembered—she'd just been saying she needed a coalition, that not everything should be about her. Maybe this was Ella's moment. She deserved that. So Dime stayed in the tree.

Layanie said, yes, it was true, Ja-lal had been in Pito. But the matter had been resolved. Ve stressed again the importance of keeping each culture separate, for the good of both. Required now to caveat each line, she reiterated that Ella was a unique case, a single visitor. And like Ella, the visitors were a blip to harmony, an incident to move past.

Yet those words did not ring true. Ella sat there, a proud, bald contradiction to every implication.

There can be no peace between us. But there was. And Ella was proving it.

Throughout, despite the hushed murmurs and whispers of wings, no one interrupted. No one left, save an occasional parent ushering out an unruly ch'pyr. The respect for the Seats was so great—so unyielding—that Dime saw how *easy* it would have been for the leaders to just speak the truth. The thing that was impossible was simply not. They simply chose not to do it.

As the speech drew to a close, Dime started to realize maybe this was it. The assembly was short. Almost over.

"Usually they will take a few questions, through the Clerk," Volana whispered, pointing down to Tikinal. In fact, Tikinal rose from his seat, turning toward the line of petitioners that had gathered.

"We wanted you to hear it from us," Ferala intoned. "Our utmost priority is your well-being and safety, surrounded here by Sha's protection."

"Sha's protection," the crowd repeated.

And then, after exchanging a few quiet words, Ferala and Layanie rose into the sky, Tikinal and several High Guards following. It was hard to say from a distance, but Dime did not see or sense Neimano's guards among them.

Only then, at the leaders' departure, did the empty sky erupt into a flutter of wings. Too many thoughts jumbled in Dime's mind, but one first among them. Gliding herself and Rock down with the aid of a springy tree branch, she rushed to where Ella stood, a mob surrounding her, including as many as five marshals, who'd clearly been sent there to escort her away. Hopefully that was all they would do.

"Ella," Dime called, flipping the hood off and into her arms, not fully reasoning through it but feeling emboldened and wanting to show support. Rock followed suit, and soon the three fe'pyrsi stood there, in the middle of the gathered crowd: Rock with her gray skin and drawn-on markings, Ella with her darker skin and weathered scalp tattoos, and Dime, feeling lost in the middle, with her short, white hair and twirling vines.

And they ignored the marshals as pyr after pyr made their way to them, asked who they were, where they were from. And they answered. That was it. They answered.

Just when Dime had almost forgotten what they'd done, as much fun as she was having meeting the curious fairies, Ella tapped her on the arm. "We've pushed enough. Time to go."

Ella turned to the marshals. "I accept High Seat Ferala's welcome, but we are leaving now. I give you my word. There is no need to follow." She turned and left.

Responding to the inherent authority of Ella's shaky voice, the marshals turned away, confused. Likewise, Dime and Rock trailed after her, noting that Uchitar and Volana had stayed with them, but were keeping a slight distance behind.

"This is Fe'Rock. And the two behind us," Dime clarified, "are my friends."

"Our friends," Rock corrected. "Uch, we go way back, don't we?" she called over her shoulder.

"Sure as Shatide," he replied, looking as cheerful as Dime had seen him. She was glad; he'd drawn away at odd intervals and Dime could only presume his absence from tzetz was distressing him.

Dime wasn't sure how far any others would follow, but they'd left suddenly, and Ella had taken a series of sharp turns around tall patches of brush. So now they stood alone, in the middle of several immense trees. Only then did Ella break expression.

"We have a way of finding each other?"

"Or a way of finding the High Seat?" Dime laughed. "Ella! What a surprise for you to be here. Are you well?"

It wasn't meant to come across as pyrsonal as it did, but it wasn't even Ella's previous depression that Dime was alluding to. More, she knew how difficult it must be for Ella to walk among the Fo-ror, seeing shadows of Suzannelina, wondering what could have been, or maybe just resenting the culture to which her spouse never felt comfortable to return. Or maybe that wasn't quite right. Or some combination. Dime didn't know how to explain it all, but she knew that Ella being here was big. And brave.

"Well? Not exactly. But I did it? Didn't I!" She wheezed. "Here, I need to sit." She eased onto a fallen tree limb, resting the stick against its side. "So the great thing about the Heartland is so few pyrsi walk down this way, it's quite easy to find a place to rest. Up there?" She pointed up into the trees. "Like midcity during festival. Here." She sighed. "It's perfect. But of course, that's the Ja-lal in me talking."

Ella paused to take a drink from her flask and rummage out a bag of nuts. "Nuts?" Everyone held out their hand except Volana, lost in thought. Crunching through the snack didn't stop Ella from continuing. "I originally was just thinking about what you said. About maybe getting some company. I didn't want to disturb your big meeting, and I never did hear whether Tum had been returned safely, so I went to check on Juni."

Likewise, Dime had tried to check in on Ella earlier, but she'd already been gone.

"As you know, Tum was fine, back with you all, and jumping squips did Juni have a lot to say about that. That cub adores every breath your child takes!" She looked over at Rock. "Have you met her children? They are wonderful."

"I met Dayn, but haven't met the children yet."

"Ah, Dayn." Ella made a comic face that brimmed with fondness. Dime really was going to have to figure out what was going on between those two.

"So after hearing the same stories from Juni for about the tenth time each, I said my farewells and decided, since I was this way anyway, to head toward the city. Didn't take me long to get the scoop. Two Ja-lal escaped prison, essentially gave the Third Seat the Soldown in front of a crowd of onlooking staff, then strolled off. Well, I knew who *that* was. At least, this one." She motioned toward Dime.

"Anyway, the chatter was blowing like grass in a windstorm. Found out pyrsi were demanding, in the polite way fairies demand, to hear from the leadership. Heard an emergency speaking event was scheduled with the High Seat. And here we are. Or . . . were?"

Dime sat down next to Ella. "I'm still shocked you're here." And happy, too. Dime was so happy to see her.

"Maybe you made me bolder. Now stop gloating about it."

"She never does," Rock said with an innocent grin.

Ella grinned back. "What are you up to here?"

Dime wasn't sure why all her friends were smirking about her like Aochs, but, being an actual grown pyr herself, she ignored it for the moment. "I came by to talk to Volana. I wanted to propose a larger plan: that Rock and I could keep working with Ador on communications in Sol's Reach, and she and Uchitar could keep working with the Foundry here. That instead of more directed talks, we could start speaking more openly. We can check up sometimes—and adjust as needed." She really had no idea why Rock was smirking again, but she continued.

"Then I wanted to check on Juni. I haven't seen her since she brought Tum back to the den. By the way, we're no longer there. I wanted to thank her and let her know I hadn't forgotten. I'd also see how Stern Eyes was doing, and the rest."

Ella's face pinched at hearing they weren't at the den anymore, likely knowing they wouldn't have left—at least not so soon—without another disruption. But she seemed more interested in the newts. "You were going to go alone? To the Beds?"

"No, with Rock." Dime knew where Ella was going with this. "I know I don't know how to speak with them yet, but I got along before. Juni knows what thanking is, if nothing else. I mostly don't want them to think I've forgotten about them. I think I can tell them I'm still trying to figure out what to do about the net."

Ella's tilted expression indicated she did not think Dime had done so well communicating with the newts, but Dime ignored it. They could really all stop piling on.

"And I talked to Uchitar and Volana about it too; they are going to ask more questions, now that this is over." She pointed back in the direction of the assembly.

"The thing with the newts," Ella said, "is it's easy to say, 'oh, they're like pyrsi.' And in many ways they are. They are also not. Their sensibilities are different. Their ethics—their lines of right and wrong. If one is different than a Ja-lal right or wrong. Or a Fo-ror"— she motioned to the fairies—"would that change our empathy? Our connection?"

"Ella?" Uchitar said the name as though unsure of it. "Most of us are several flaps behind what you suggest. I've never even heard newts and ethics in the same conversation."

"I know," Ella nodded. "That's why I'm offering that caution. Don't make them have to be like us to be worthy of our respect. Or their autonomy." Ella seemed pleased at the thoughtfully bobbing heads surrounding her. "What a wonderful group you are. You are tugging at me, whether you know it or not, to stay a while longer."

"You're welcome as long as you want," Volana said, curving her fingers.

"I know, friend." Ella returned the gesture. "Thank you. But I have someone I need to tend to, and this night was . . . a lot. I need some time. Alone."

"Would you like me to help you back to Sol's Reach? I'm used to the valence now." Dime tapped her pendant, under her shirt.

"Sol, no!" Without rising, she tapped her walking stick. "That help, I do not need."

Rock chortled, to Dime's growing exasperation.

Realizing she'd gone a little far, Rock threw her an apologetic smile, which Dime accepted.

"Oh, I was kidding," Ella said with a dismissive wave. "I know a pair who'll drive me back. I can even sleep on the way." As Ella had turned wes, Dime assumed that meant she was going to the Crossing, and would hire a ride from there.

"Accompany you for a bit more?" Dime offered.

"I'd like that," Ella said with a warm, but tired, smile.

They walked with Ella until she said they'd taken her far enough. There, Volana added, she had to check on the creeks; she was overdue.

"You'll go back home?" Volana asked Uchitar. "Directly?"

"Yes," he answered, an edge to his tone.

"I need you to promise."

For once, Uchitar did not look so pleasant, and Dime felt uneasy.

"I promise," he said, flying up into the trees without a look back.

"It's so hard, Dime." Volana didn't look like she wanted a response and so Dime didn't offer one.

Forcing her mouth into a smile, Volana turned and offered a muttered goodbye. "Your plan is good. I'm sure I'll see you again. You know where to leave word."

Dime nodded, feeling an unexpected sadness as Volana lifted back up and away.

"Go see some newts?" Rock offered. "Take your mind off all of it?"

Dime had almost forgotten Rock was still there. "Yeah," she said. "Sure."

"This way?" Rock pointed.

"It's easier by chair, so we have to go back to Volana's."

"D, I'm not doing the chair thing—"

"I know—Volana said you could take one of hers. I can lift both; I've done so before." She didn't like balancing multiple chairs, but it would work. This time, she thought she could control them separately, as long as she kept Rock's close by. "Sorry, it won't have a full back, but it does have arm rests."

"Great! Well, uh, I had an idea. If you can lift wood chairs, why not just lift us?"

"I'm too nervous to try. That's—too far."

"Alright. Our clothes?"

Dime leaned her head over. "I want you to think about that for two strides."

"Oh. Good point." Rock pulled a long grimace. "Well, let's walk back to Volana's?"

"Actually, I did want to try something. In case we get in a pinch."

Rock whooped in the silliest ways as, together, they lifted a stick in the air between them and hung from it as it rose up and sped back in the direction of Volana's house, which fortunately, wasn't too far away. Dime kept concentrating, not just to hold on but to keep the stick steady and out of the way of oncoming obstacles. She was relieved when they set down on Volana's walkway, and she collapsed down, tossing the stick over the edge.

"See, that climbing . . . paid off," Rock wheezed, plopping down and rubbing her arms. "And we're not doing that again either . . . unless we have to."

Dime saw that Volana, or maybe Uchitar, had already set the extra chair outside, next to Dime's. "Should we—" Dime was looking at the entrance curtain. Surely Uchitar was inside by now.

Rock shook her head. "Trust me. Let's just go. He doesn't want us looking in on him. He'll be fine. He promised Volana directly. Would take a while for that to wear off."

"How do you know?"

Rock wasn't smiling. "I do. Now, let's go, before we distract him."

There wasn't any ceremony or giggling this time. Feeling it an old task, Dime made sure Rock was holding her own chair tightly, then they both lifted up into the air, and off again.

"Harm it," she muttered.

"What is it?"

Dime wasn't going to turn to look at Rock, but she sounded worried. "Someone is following us."

"How do you know, D?"

"I can feel it."

Interlude

Her teacher's words rang in Cisebale's head the entire flight home.

"I'm sure you misunderstood," she'd said. "This is our Director you're talking about. He's been a great influence on all of music since well before your birth. Music he composed has been played in the chambers of the Seats!"

Cisebale knew the orchestra Director was good at music. She knew he brought joy into pyrsi's lives. And she didn't think that's what she was saying.

She'd even tried again. She'd repeated her story, word for word. She'd exaggerated only a little, and only the second time, hoping her teacher would listen.

"It sounds like you misunderstood," she'd said. "Ok? Now, go along; your family will wonder why you're not back."

This season's teacher didn't know anything about her family. Whether she went straight home or not. What shifts they worked. And so the teacher's words felt hollow. Not a lie—lying would be the Violence. But something . . . didn't feel right.

Thumping down past the curtain, Cisebale tossed her bag onto a cushion, and headed back to the space she shared with her sibling. He was there with one of his friends, engaged in a lively game of wrist ball, which they were supposed to play outside. She sat down, trying to ignore their shouts back and forth.

"Cisebale?" Her parther was home, though her teacher wouldn't have known that. Ve called out from the main room, where Cisebale had fluttered past. But of course, Pa-pa always knew when something was wrong.

Something was wrong. It was.

"Yeah?" she answered, hoping to avoid going back out. Maybe ve couldn't hear her over the din of the ma'ch'pyrsi's playing.

"Come out here, please."

Wings pulling tight, Cisebale dragged out.

Pa-pa was knitting in a chair, vis ankles casually crossed over the plush rug. "Something wrong?"

"I'm not sure. It was a . . . long shift at classes."

Pa-pa set down vis needles. "Yes, that can happen. If you need to talk, you let me know."

She shrugged, turning back toward the bedroom.

"Anytime," Pa-pa added.

Cisebale went back into the room.

Perhaps this was a bad choice. Her sibling was being so loud, and his new friend was worse. Maybe she could fly uptree and work on some music. At seven cycles old, some would give her the eye for being there alone, but she knew the right places to go.

Except, music didn't feel so nice right now.

The words rang in her mind. She misunderstood. Director was successful. Cisebale was only a ch'pyr.

Maybe she shouldn't have said anything at all.

One. One more time.

She dragged back out. "Pa-pa?"

Her parther motioned for her to sit. Cisebale glanced over at the doorway. Maybe she should just go.

"Sometimes the bravest thing we can do," ve said in a low tone, "is say it."

Cisebale turned to the wall. "At classes, the orchestra Director has made me feel uncomfortable. He . . . asks me to take off my cloak. Says it makes it difficult to move my bow." Cisebale liked to wear dip-back robes, but Pa-pa would know that. She didn't like the feel of fabric against her wings while flying, so she wore short dip-back robes. But she didn't want to be too plain at classes, so she always put on a cloak with little sparkles on it. Once she got there.

She thought she looked cool that way.

By the look on Pa-pa's face, she regretted saying anything. "It might be my fault," she amended. "I asked him his attractions once. Not, like, details or anything—of course—but I was just curious. I like to know pyrsi. I know I shouldn't have asked that."

"Is it . . . normal to remove a cloak while playing?"

See, even Pa-pa thought she was making something of it. "The first chair doesn't have to. But he's a ma'ch'pyr." And Director had answered her. He said he'd only 'been with' fe'pyrsi. That wasn't what Cisebale had asked him, though. She'd asked his attractions. Not who he'd 'been with.'

"It seemed weird when he asked me," she continued. "And I took it off the first time, because he's Director. But then he asked it again and I didn't think it made sense. I . . . said something to my teacher, and she said I probably misunderstood."

Pa-pa leaned forward, tucking vis knitting back into vis waist. "Sometimes the bravest thing someone can do," ve said, "is to speak. And her premise is false. Even misunderstandings need to be addressed. Especially when they are not. Thank you. We will figure this out. I promise."

Cisebale stepped toward her room, then turned around. "I'm worried about going back to orchestra now." She hoped that wasn't a weak thing to say. But she was. Maybe it would be worse now.

"I know," Pa-pa said, vis voice gentle. "That's what made it brave."

Act 3

POLYPHONY

Rock braced herself as Dime lowered both chairs to the forest floor. They were far outside the city now, as Dime had been heading toward the netting. And so, surrounded by forest and no sign of homes above, she felt certain they were three alone: Rock, herself, and whoever had followed them.

"Who's there?" Dime called into the trees. "I know you're there, and I'm not leaving until I find out who followed us."

A glowstone was lit, illuminating a tall fairy with an uneasy smirk plastered on xyr face. Dime had an immediate sense, well, that this was a pyr with problems.

Xe was well-put together, with short, almost tunic-length robes that allowed free movement of xyr long, narrow wings. A soft, plain pant fell underneath. Xyr hair was dyed black and pulled into long twists, and a cord draped around xyr neck, carrying a forged metal pendant. Though xe wore sleeves, xyr build had a muscular appearance. By xyr skin, xe was much older than herself or Rock. Yet it wasn't xyr appearance that raised a banner for Dime; it was the odd, forced expression on xyr face.

"I'm Fe'Diamond," she said. Rock bristled. Then, Rock wasn't going to introduce herself.

The pyr didn't seem concerned. "Ma'Intinpalo," he returned

with the curved finger gesture. "I thought I saw more brutes join the other one, and at first, I was interested to see what you were up to."

"You're more than interested," Dime said, as Rock stood silent beside her. "Come on, what's your angle here? Are you with the Seats? The Foundry?" Perhaps his metal necklace was symbolic. Though, Volana didn't wear any metal that Dime could remember.

He rolled his eyes. "The Foundry stands for nothing. Just talk— talk that does no good for anyone. Nothing's better and some things are worse. Sitting around and talking about it does nothing."

"Then who are you with?" Rock asked, her voice terse.

"The Risers. An old group. Respected." He walked right up, pulling his gaze away from Dime's face to inspect their wooden chairs. "I almost thought you had better contraptions than they say." He ducked down and squinted through his lamplight, as though trying to find a mechanism.

"Yeah. We do," Rock quipped. "Flying chairs and all. Now, do you have anything to say to us? Because if not, we were just on our way."

"I have plenty to say. One of you is a Fo-ror and I'm curious which." He glanced up at Dime's hair. "You, then?"

"Sure, I am." Dime wasn't sure why she said it. She supposed it went back to her pledge against hiding. Demanding to know some-one's pyrsonal details was a form of the Violence. But who knew, she felt like answering him, and she wasn't going to stand here and make up some story about how the chairs flew. Besides, he'd probably felt the valence. So he knew anyway.

"I'm also a Ja-lal," she added. "Now, tell us about the Risers." Dime felt odd being quippy with a stranger, but his pitched syllables and aggressive stares set a tone that was contagious.

"Want to tell me your story? What happened to your wings? How you tattooed yourself? Why you have neither proper hair nor brutish grooming?"

"Nope, I don't," Dime answered. She'd asked him a question.

Volana had mentioned the Risers in a negative light, she remembered, but Dime still didn't understand their full intent.

"Well. Maybe you'll change your mind. You see, I'd like your help. The Risers are not against her kind." He motioned to Rock, whose face was impassively locked. "I've dreamed about visiting the Barrens—Sol's Reach is what you call them, right? Even the name is beautiful. See, the Seats don't want pyrsi to discuss the truth. They want us to revere the Heartland and not even name the rest. To say it's perfect here, when it's not. There's sadness, and crowding, and—" He cut his eyes to the side. "A lot of us want something better."

His voice grew in intensity. "Think about how close Sol's Reach is to here. Yet we're forbidden to fly there. Filled with stories about how awful it is, to make sure we don't try. Why? Maybe . . . just maybe they don't want us to know the truth about it. How great it is. If the Fo-ror are Sha's pyrsi, why would we only inhabit half the land? Unless someone was keeping us from it."

"Come on, let's go," Rock murmured, not taking her eyes off the pyr. "I'll tell you more when we leave."

Dime also worried where he was going with this speech, but she wasn't going to just leave without trying to find out more. Especially since the pyr knew her secret. Part of it, anyway. They were here to build a coalition, and she didn't yet know who might provide information they needed—or even be swayed to help. At least maybe she'd learn something.

"So I'm curious what you'll do when you to go to Sol's Reach. Live amongst the Ja-lal, I presume? By their rules? Would you form a separate society among us? Or try to merge our two cultures into something new?"

Intinpalo's eyes flickered. "It could be a time to reorganize the nature of the Seats, yes. And I put great trust in you by mentioning that." He stepped forward to accentuate the point. Dime stepped back, almost bumping against Rock.

"You didn't mention the Circles," Dime noted, stepping to her friend's side. "Our government. You'd need to work with them as well, and with other organizations I know. I have a friend—"

"Stop," Rock growled, and as close as they were, Dime could feel her tensing. "Why are we telling this pyr anything? You're naïve. He's a supremacist, just a different flavor. He wants the Fo-ror to take over Sol's Reach."

Dime snapped around to look at her friend. Rock's expression was disconcerting, angry even, but Dime was trying to sort all this in her head, and understand what the pyr was saying. Wasn't that their job? To learn? Talking? Voice? Hadn't they just had this whole conversation?

But Rock was upset and Dime wasn't going to ignore her. "Well, let's ask him." She turned to Intinpalo, who was glaring determinedly at Rock. Dime didn't like the look; she tried to get his attention. "Do the Risers intend to disrupt the Ja-lal?"

"You're not one of them," he whispered, slowly turning over. "Whatever has been done to you, I'm sorry, but this is just making our point. We wish the . . . Ja-lal . . . no ill. We'll provide for them as well."

Dime blinked.

Rock flung up a hand. "See?" She threw Dime a cutting glance, while not taking her focus from Intinpalo. "And what if the Ja-lal say no to this plan? You do it anyway? Return the Violence? Blame us?"

"No!" Intinpalo nearly snarled. "We're against the Violence. But Sha's pyrsi should not be confined within its lands. It's wrong. With governance over Ada-ji, everyone will be happier. Better taken care of. We'll share Ada-ji's resources among *all*. This would be good for you." He was staring at Rock, irritation in his eyes.

As Rock turned back to Dime, her eyes blazing, Dime suddenly knew what a huge mistake she'd just made. She couldn't say she understood it, but a misstep was clear. This wasn't fair—a stranger accosts them, she's trying to figure it all out, and Rock expects her to be perfect. But Rock was livid and Dime needed to fix it.

She swung back to Intinpalo. "If you're going to talk to my friend that way, then I'm leaving. Whatever you thought you found back there, you didn't find it. I'm Ja-lal, and Sol's Reach is not some waiting prize.

"I'm willing to talk to your group if you're willing to listen, but not like this. And not at all if you're going to talk down to my friend. When you want to talk, you let me know. You don't follow me in a forest. You communicate with me, and we'll sit down and we'll talk about both societies working together. Together. Not one telling the other what's best for them."

The curl to Intinpalo's lip made it clear he knew Dime was not going to help him that night. Good. She wasn't.

"You're affected by them," he whispered, as if Rock couldn't hear it.

"Of course I am. And you're affected by a lifetime of absorbing a myth, one meant to deceive. And promoting it, sounds like. Well I'm sorry. But I can't correct you right now, and I don't have to. Now let us leave."

"I'm sorry," she murmured to Rock. "Let's go."

They walked toward the chairs, but Rock stayed standing, folding her arms and staring indistinctly away from them both.

"Leave us alone," Dime hollered, and Intinpalo, with a look of disgust, flew back up into the trees.

Rock spun to meet her gaze. "Were you going to tell him everything? Some randafairy shows up in the forest, then says he's part of a harm group—you tell him your history, you out the Foundry, you almost brought in Ador—are you thinking about any of this?"

"No! I'm not thinking about it. Some pyr finds us when we're trying to leave, says he's from an organization I don't know anything about—Volana never told us much; how do I know they're harmful—and could sense my valence. He felt it. I can't hide that. What was I supposed to do?"

"I was *right here*. We're a team. You promised. Did you listen at all? You ignored me and started spouting off details that he didn't need to know. Maybe you don't know about the Risers, but I do. I'm in Dawn's Circle, remember? I've studied them. How about pull me aside first. 'Rock, what do you think? Since we're a team.'"

Dime threw up a hand. "We are a team. But you expect me to be perfect and I'm not. Or I'm supposed to immediately know whether someone is harmful, when *all* of us have been misinformed. He felt my valence; how am I supposed to hide that? And I didn't 'spout' any details; I have no idea what you're talking about."

"You're missing the point."

"Well, maybe you need to tell me the point, because I can't be worried about tripping over it every time someone figures out who I am."

Rock's eyes grew wide. She was reading into something. What did Dime say? She hadn't done anything wrong, and—

"You better take Volana back her chair," she snapped, turning and stomping off through the trees.

"Rock, please. Come back." Dime felt the strands rip from her, pulling into the forest, as her friend stormed away. Out of sight, into the dark. With Rock's skill, Dime could never find her. And what was she supposed to do, chase her as Intinpalo had chased them? Rock was her own pyr. "Please come back," she said, then, after a long pause, shouting as loud as she could. "Rock!"

How was she supposed to keep doing this? She had a strange enough road, and everyone was affected. Poor Dayn. Her children. Ella. Ador. Hin. Pyrsi were the one thing that kept her moving. And yet Dime was supposed to tiptoe over every breath to make sure she didn't offend some unspoken ruleset. It was exhausting. She couldn't do it.

She collapsed into the dirt and sat there a really long time. It felt like a really long time. There was nothing left. No breath. No ability to stand. No ability to think. And so, when the fairy landed back in front of her with his conciliatory tone, she had nothing for him. Vapors, only.

"Look, you seem nice," he said.

Glad you think so. "I'm not in the mood to deal with this. Don't talk to me. But, come, I'm going to show you where we were going."

It was a strange notion, one that popped into her head. Rock wouldn't have liked it. But Rock wasn't there. Rock left. And they were going to see the net, so she was going to show someone the killmaster *net*.

Intinpalo said nothing as Dime took rope from her bag, lashed Volana's chair to the side of her own, sat down, and flew up into the night. She heard the flapping of his wings behind her, but she made no attempt to look back. And she flew wes, knowing she would see it soon, reaching out with the energy within her necklace. Speeding faster now.

Then, it was there. Dime set herself down. Not having worn the strap Ella made, she popped up from her chair and turned to face the intruding fairy.

"*This,*" she yelled, stomping over toward the net. "This. The net. I'm sure you've heard of it, but this is what it looks like. This harmstinked, diamond-infused net keeps the newts away from their home, their food, their water, their way of life. You think Fo-ror are better than Ja-lal? You think they are better than the newts? It's dung. If you were better, you'd help them, not harm them. So you want to do something? You want to do something? You do something about *this.*" She shook the net like it would bring Rock back, like it would take her to Dayn, like it would protect her children, like she could just wake up in her bed and not have to deal with anything that had happened, from being different than everyone else, and having her life constantly disrupted for it.

"The net protects us," he said, seeming to be fumbling for words.

"Protects you? You want to be protected, *you* live in a net. You don't just keep everyone out, like you have more of a right to be here than anyone else."

"Sha grants—"

"Sha's pyrsi, right?" She'd heard the same thing in Lodon: the

Ja-lal were Sol's pyrsi. "The light and the water chose us? That's pretty grand. Well, maybe the animals belong to Sha too. Maybe we're just . . . fancy animals."

"We aren't like *animals*," Intinpalo sputtered, as if the idea was more absurd than offensive. "We reason and build, and are granted valence."

"And you use all that to do this?" Dime gave the ropes a final shake. "Would you be so impressive without your diamonds?" she added. In that moment, she almost did it again. She almost tore the harmed-off diamond from her neck and stomped it into the ground. But something Rock had said stayed her hand. She didn't even remember what. She just . . . didn't do it.

Intinpalo stood like a statue, the bottom of his short robe flapping rapidly in the breeze. He didn't even look at the net. "I forgot to ask you; you said I could contact you again. How?"

Dime snorted. "You can talk to the Foundry."

She was glad for Intinpalo's disgusted look, and glad when, without a farewell, he launched off into the sky. This time, she knew, he wouldn't come back.

Overwhelmed and not wanting to admit the one thing she wanted right now, she collapsed against the net and cried.

She heard the howl in her thoughts, like the sound of a newt. That's right, she was going to visit them. And she still should; Rock would probably show up there and things would be fine. *Hrm.* Had she fallen asleep? The howl sounded again.

"Ma-ma?" A voice rang out. "Luja, look, over there, it's Ma-ma."

This was not in her thoughts. But, what? She rose, confused.

"Ma-ma!"

Dime blinked at the shapes that appeared before her: Juni holding Tum in her arms, and Luja swinging a small lamp in vis hand. Tum and Luja were both agape, and Juni looked ready to drop Tum in her excitement.

"She smelled you, but I didn't believe her," Tum said, leaning forward.

Before her children could notice it, Dime tried to shake off her fog. Gathering herself, she flipped back through the events of the last turns. Tum and Luja were hidden at the hut, in the old woods. Not bounding through the forest of the Heartland with Juni. And not *inside* the netting. Yet her disbelief was overshadowed by the group standing right in front of her. "Wow!" she managed to stammer. "How are you here? How did you get inside the net?"

Setting down the lamp, Luja whipped a pickaxe from vis side. Dime recognized it as one they'd taken from the den. "We dug!" Ve lowered the tool. "Actually, I didn't need it. Juni's the digger here. All the newts are. They're just used to digging roots and burrows, not tunneling through. I showed them how to do it. With safety precautions!" Vis eyes narrowed.

"Safety? You were supposed to stay safe at the hut," Dime said, still stunned. But they were here; she could see them. "This isn't following the rules at all." She glanced back and forth at her children's grins.

"We did learn it from you," Luja said, raising vis shoulders up with a tilt of vis head. "And besides, that hut was awful."

"Ok. Awful hut. I tried." She tried not to think how long it had taken them to build it. "But—how did you get out?" She remembered the steep ledges of the old woods; Tum couldn't scale those, even if the others could. "And where is your father?"

"It was all Tum's idea!"

Tum beamed beside ver.

"I mean, we left like one bell after you did. We were all sort of sitting there and it was peaceful and nice and no one was shouting at us, but how can we enjoy peaceful and nice if you're out there helping pyrsi? So instead of going up, we went down. We couldn't take Tum's chair, but we went slowly, and Sha wasn't actually that far away."

Sha. Her face must have shown her surprise.

"Yes! I know! Ga-da Gorg told Tum a story once about floating on water using a mat. So we built a mat, and it worked, and we could paddle really fast. We got to the Beds pretty quickly, while it was still day. Juni was so surprised!" Ve reached over and patted Juni's arm.

"Lu, she asked about Da-da too," Tum broke in. "He's at the Beds! Building a new common area that's more sheltered."

"But still lets air flow through," Luja added, as always concerned about wellness.

Juni let out a whimper.

"Oh, she thinks we're ignoring her," Dime said, realizing as she said it that perhaps she had been. "I'm sorry, Juni, I don't know how to speak to you like Ella does." Ella, after all, had lived with the newts for what sounded like a long time, both that first time, and then visiting over the course of several cycles. Dime had just been there a couple of turns. Still, she should get over there and offer her a hug, she supposed. No licking, though.

A second whimper sounded, similar, but not from Juni. And Dime almost stumbled realizing where it came from. *Tum.* Though it had the sound of being stilted, it was clear that Tum was filling Juni in on the conversation.

"She's really good at it," Luja whispered.

Dime watched in amazement. "I have a little food," she finally said. "Want to sit down for a while?"

Not wanting to sit in the shadow of the net, they moved away from it, Dime using valence to lift the chairs in front of them as they walked, much to Juni's delight.

Dime hadn't packed any meals, but she divided up the last bit of snacks she carried and passed each handful around.

"So how have you been doing?" Luja asked, amidst Juni's happy grunts. "I didn't expect you to be here; we thought you were in Lodon."

They didn't expect me to be here? she thought.

"I was," she said instead. "I talked to the Light and then Jaza, the leader of Sol's Pillars."

What, Luja mouthed.

Dime couldn't help but grin. "Yes. I thought it was a pretty productive schedule myself, though I can't say it went as I hoped. So we flew down here—well, a friend of mine was with me a while, but now it's me." She pushed away the pang she felt, hastening her words. "We listened to the High and Second Seats speak, and oh, I have a story about that that you'll love. Then we met with another faction, sort of— And, here I am."

Luja's mouth pulled over, and ve lowered vis fruit stick.

"What?" Dime knew that expression.

"Why is your friend a secret?"

"Secret? I don't have a secret friend. What are you talking about?" She'd mentioned that Rock was there for a while; it was no secret.

"You never say 'my friend,' you say, 'hey I'm going out with Ador,' or 'hey Zael and Yorm are meeting us for some music thing.' You don't say 'a friend was with me.'"

Dime sighed. "Her name's Rock. We used to work together. She's someone I really trust."

"Why didn't you say her name, then?"

For a moment, Dime wondered why she hadn't. But, it was obvious. And it irritated her beyond the moment she was going to admit this to an Aoch. "We got in a tiff after getting here. We'd *agreed* to stick together. She'd agreed to be part of our efforts, and I was grateful that she was. It just . . . got off on the wrong foot and we kept bumping helmets after that. Anyway, she took some things the wrong way, or, I mean, maybe I said some things the wrong way, *which happens,* and she stomped off."

Luja raised vis eyebrows.

For some reason, and she couldn't deny the oddness of the reversal, she felt like unloading. "I'm frustrated, ok? Ever since I left the hut, and I mean, why did we build it then? Ever since I left the hut, I've realized that the key to making a change is getting more pyrsi informed and involved. If this . . . ordeal started with secrets and confusion, then it needs to end with openness and resolve. So I've been trying to do that.

"I feel great about Volana and Ador agreeing to help, and I thought maybe I could help too. But Sala brushed me off. Jaza just went on about turning pyrsi against the fairies, which was never even Sol's Pillars' thing until now, which I guess is what this last pyr's after too. I mean, he's a fairy, but he thought I'd help the fairies charge into Sol's Reach without a plan except 'taking over.' He doesn't even claim to dislike us, just thinks fairies ought to be in charge, which is gross. Oh, and I saw Ferala again, and I thought that would be an opportunity, but then it just wasn't the right place to interfere.

"I can't get anything done. I think I sort of know what I'm supposed to do, but it's always a windstorm—out there and in my mind too—I keep getting swept side-to-side." She sighed. "It's not just like . . . a clear path forward."

"It usually isn't like that," was Luja's response. "Except in stories."

Juni, now free of having Tum in her arms, exhaled along with Dime as she hopped over and swept Dime up. Murmuring, she ran her fingers across Dime's hair as though comforting her. Or maybe it was grooming, but she was going with comforting.

"Yes, Juni, you're wonderful." The embrace was sort of nice, but she couldn't let her children see her snuggle in like a ba'pyr. Still, she didn't try to escape right away. Soon, she swung herself back to the ground, resting a hand on the scales of Juni's arm. "Tum, tell her I'm so glad to see her."

Tum murmured something, and Juni grunted. For a stride, it almost looked like she was going to lick her, but their eyes met in understanding. Instead she reached her arms out. Dime was shocked to see the newt offering her the bridge. She hurried to take it, though once their arms connected, Juni pulled in a little closer than was proper, her chest feathers tickling Dime's face. Releasing, she stepped back. "Thank you, Juni. For understanding."

"I think if you don't like being pulled side-to-side then start pushing forward," Luja said.

Dime paused. "Well, I've been trying. But you're right, maybe I need to try harder."

"Did you think it would be easy?"

She almost scolded ver for talking back, but vis tone was encouraging, not disrespectful. And Luja was getting almost too old for Dime's scolding, anyway. Time for ver to live vis life. That caught her breath a little, like a river had just opened between them. No, not a river. Just some air. And that was alright.

"No," Dime replied. "I didn't think it would be anything. I didn't plan for any of this. But easy, no, it never crossed my mind." She offered ver a smile, which ve returned, calming her.

She noticed her youngest staring up at her. "What do you think, Tum? You've been quiet." Admittedly, the ch'pyr had downed a whole wrapping of crackers, which probably made it hard to talk, but it was still unlike Tum to say so little.

"I need to talk to Juni," she said. Moving over next to the newt, Tum switched back into the newt language, Juni responding in kind.

Dime waited as the two continued to chatter, and she watched them with amazement. And her amazement turned to concern as the tone of their conversation shifted, the two repeating the same sounds as if trying to understand. Finally, Tum turned toward her.

"We made an agreement. So I can tell you something."

Dime had no idea what that meant.

"Some of the newts are growing ill. It's a reaction to the water, but it didn't used to happen. Some sort of condition that makes them feel tired and sick."

Dime could see Juni understood what Tum was conveying, even if she couldn't understand the words. "Tell her I'm sorry," she said.

"Oh, she knows already by your face. But it's really upsetting the troop of course, not only this troop but up and down the sand. And—" Tum spoke again to Juni as if making a final confirmation.

"Their Leader is considering . . . returning to Home Sha. Even—" Tum drew her face. "Even if that means using . . . the Violence to get the flying two-legs to let them stay. Sorry, I mean the fairies. Sorry, I mean the Fo-ror."

Dime tried not to react, but her mind was spinning. She'd spent so much time worrying about the Ja-lal and the Fo-ror returning the Violence, she'd never considered— Also, if Tum and Juni had made a deal, it just sounded like Tum had told her everything. Dime wondered what the deal could be. This worried her, too.

"Could it be soon?" she asked.

If so, they'd have to do something. Dime had no idea what.

"Juni says no," Tum answered. "It sounds like kind of a whispery thing. Nothing would happen without some big meeting. But I still told Juni it was important to tell you."

"Tell her thank you." Dime paused, her chest heavy. "Let's go back to the Beds and discuss it," she said. "I was planning on going anyway. We can tell the troop that we're trying to help. Without letting them know what Juni said, of course."

"Umm . . ." Luja fidgeted.

Dime raised her eyebrows.

"Da-da's got it taken care of. You're working on Sol's Reach, right? I assume Volana's leading things here? You were probably, you know, checking in? I mean, Tum can talk to the newts, and Da-da and I are helping."

"Ma-ma, we're not staying at the hut while you go around and help," Tum added, her eyes as earnest as Luja's were concerned. "I mean, I don't mean that in a rude way."

"I know you don't," she murmured, reaching out for a hug, which Tum accepted.

Tum never meant anything in a rude way. She was a unique spirit, and Dime tried to sort through a swirl of emotions. She couldn't stop spinning on Tum's warning, nor did she know how to deal with it. The newts returning to Home Sha—which would be seen as the Violence however it was done—would justify everything the Fo-ror had done to them. It would in Fo-ror minds. She released Tum, who walked back to Juni's side.

Dime noticed Luja was staring at her, and Dime wondered what ve was thinking.

"Tum," ve finally said. "Show her the other stuff."

"Show her what? We've done a lot."

"I know, but you're better. Show her your colors."

Now, Dime really had no idea what that meant. And they should have warned her, because a parent's instinct set in the moment that her child's face began to change. Though each change was imperceptible, it took its course quickly, as Tum's skin, still very light at her age, grew . . . green? Yes, greenish, then darker, fading into the tree behind her until her angular neckline, edged in the cute powder blue of her shirt, stood out, almost as if the tree were wearing it. Beside her Juni leapt up, bouncing in a broad circle around them and laughing, at least the newt sound Dime had taken to be laughing.

As Tum returned to her normal self, gasping and panting in a way that alarmed Dime entirely—though Luja seemed unconcerned—she giggled. "I can't change my clothes. Maybe you could. I'm not sure."

Dime wasn't changing anyone's clothes. But what had Tum just done? No, I mean, she was right here and saw it. Her ba'pyr. Turning colors.

Maybe she should have felt only pride for her child, but so much was changing, and Dime felt a moment of trepidation for what it all meant. She needed to remember that as she spread word of both cultures—that it wasn't always the change that was frightening, it was the untraversed pathways it opened up.

"Ma-ma?" Tum had one arm braced against the ground. The other she had raised in question. Juni was also staring at Dime.

"Oh! Yes, we'll I'm stunned. So—valence. Wow. Tum, you're really good! I can't believe it." She actually still couldn't. "And you, Luja, you too?"

"I've been working on other things, as who would change a face that looked like this?" Ve swept a hand across it. "I've been trying to see better, hear better. It'll help me in my training. As for other things, I don't need them."

Dime knew what ve meant. Equal to the pull of exploring what valence could do was the idea maybe pyrsi'd be happier with what they had already. She supposed that was a decision each pyr had to make for xemself.

"Tum's better at it, anyway. I can kind of see beyond the room, like we're in a room and there are hallways beyond it and I'm pretty ok to stay here. Tum? She races off like she knew what was there all along. She's really good. I mean, how do you think she speaks so well with the newts?"

Tum didn't hear the last part, as she'd leaned over and was talking to Juni again. But, could that be possible? Did valence help Tum learn to communicate so quickly? Ella had learned to communicate, but Ella had presumably lived with the newts a long time. She wondered whether Ella had used valence to bridge any gaps, or even if she *knew* that she had.

"Is there anything else?" Dime said to Luja, admittedly just staring blankly at her children and the newt. "Any other big news?"

"That's the basics." Luja shrugged.

"Oh, and," Dime lowered her voice to a whisper, "Agni?" Tum hadn't been carrying the kita, but then, she often didn't. Agni had her own streak of independence she didn't like to be too bruised.

"She's fine. Back with Da-da. She even went on the water with us; once Tum wraps her in that shawl, she cuddles in like she'd never leave."

Dime was glad to hear that, at least. She yawned, feeling overwhelmed. They'd all been through a lot; maybe they should get some sleep before setting back out. Just as she was about to suggest it, she noticed an uneasy twitch to Juni's nose. Dime might not have language valence, but she knew someone was worried when she saw it.

"Juni? What is it? Tum?"

"She says someone is coming," Tum whispered. "She won't say who."

"Someone is coming, like we need to leave?" Dime glanced around.

Juni plopped down again, pushing her hands against the feathers of her upper arms, like a ch'pyr who'd been caught. And with a grin, Dime had a sudden sense who was about to arrive.

Sure enough, Stern Eyes came bounding through the trees, making a chattering noise as she brushed the dirt from her feathers. Unsurprised to see Dime—but of course she'd smelled her here, and no, Dime wasn't used to that yet—Stern Eyes leapt toward her first, not even throwing a glance at still-pouting Juni.

Dime braced as Stern Eyes' wide tongue swept across her face. "Oh, yes, thank you." She reached over and rubbed her feathers. "It's so good to see you, er—

"Tum, please ask what would be more respectful to call her. I can't just keep calling her 'Stern Eyes.'"

Tum, Juni, and Stern Eyes conferred a minute, and Dime could see the newts struggling to understand what Tum was asking. Then they all chuckled, and Tum turned back to Dime. "Ok, this is a little hard to explain. She is bragging about how good her name is." Tum lowered her voice substantially on the word *good*.

"What? She wants me to call her Goo—"

"No!" her children said in unison, each waving an arm forward.

"Tum, I'll tell her," Luja said with authority. "So, the word that we say for something we like, the one we're not going to say right now, sounds really similar to their . . . mating call."

"What?" Dime stopped. "No, don't repeat it, I heard you."

"Just don't call her that," Luja continued. "The newts have a thing with names." Tum nodded. "Their name changes over time based on their standing with the troop. So anyway, Stern Eyes is really proud of hers."

"Well, what do I call her then?"

Luja looked over at Tum, who giggled.

"She likes 'Stern Eyes' a lot. She took it as a huge compliment, from what I could gather."

Indeed, Dime tried not to grin as she faced the two seated newts, their thick, scaly legs bent in front of them. Juni's eyes were bouncing back and forth, trying to read everyone's expressions. And Stern Eyes had scrunched her mouth and narrowed her eyes. Dime lowered her head a touch in deference, and Stern Eyes' expression broke. She threw an unmistakably gloating glance at Juni, then settled back against her arms.

Trying not to let her amusement show, Dime gave in and felt relieved and happy to be among friends, setting the heavier topics aside. For a bit, at least. And it made her realize how ticked off she was at Rock. Rock should have been here, meeting her children—who could use a role model like Rock—and meeting the newts. And with all Rock's research, she could have checked out the net too. Given her thoughts.

Well, she wasn't going to let that bring her down. Putting a smile on her face, she looked around at the other four. "I'm happy to be here with you."

Juni bounced in her seat, and overhead, one of the branches rattled.

Dime glanced up to see a squip watching them from over a leafy branch. Dime waved, and the squip curled out of view. "Tum, can you tell them what I've been trying to do? Getting pyrsi to talk so the Ja-lal and Fo-ror can work together toward a peaceful arrangement."

Tum told them, and while Dime couldn't vouch for the accuracy of the translation, she was concerned when she saw the newts' reactions. Or at least, Stern Eyes'. Juni was mostly just interested, interrupting and asking questions back. Maybe not questions. Clarifications, perhaps, by their tone.

But Stern Eyes grunted and drew her arms in, and the brief comradery they'd all felt here faded. Dime considered this in the context of what Tum had told her—that the newts were considering returning to Home Sha, even if they had to use the Violence. Dime wouldn't address that directly, but since the older newt was here, Dime might as well ask her what was upsetting her.

"Please ask Stern Eyes why she doesn't like pyrsi working together. Tell her maybe if we work together, we can find a way to return Home Sha."

Almost as if she'd already understood the question, there was something like incredulity in the newt's expression. She started thumping one of her hands against the ground, and Tum struggled to keep up. Juni scooted back, then covered her face with her hands.

Dime didn't know how Stern Eyes would feel that Tum and Juni had told the secret. Hopefully she hadn't said too much already.

"The fairies are keeping the newts away from Home Sha," Tum translated. "The wingless want to work with them? What about us? You should not trust the winged . . . two-legs."

"What about me?" Dime asked, pointing at herself so the meaning was clear. "You trust me."

Stern Eyes snapped something back.

Tum hesitated. "I'm not exactly sure. I think she said you like everyone."

No, Dime knew exactly what she meant by that. She sighed. "Tell her I think I understand. But if she agrees things aren't working now, and I know she does, then I'd like her help getting everyone together to talk about it."

I'd like her help? A voice in Dime's mind reminded her she was asking an animal for help, but the characterization offended her, seeing the emotion in Stern Eyes' punctuated movements. So often now, these two voices argued inside her. One reacting based on what she'd always been taught, and one reacting to what she could experience and see herself.

Stern Eyes pulled up taller as Tum repeated what Dime had said. Dime had the distinct idea she was trying to make her eyes appear sterner. It was a simple reaction, but were pyrsi really so much more complex? Even the Light wore platform shoes to try and appear taller. That wasn't so much more evolved, once she considered it.

"Tell Stern Eyes, and Juni," she added, "to find peace on Ada-ji we'll need everyone's help. Everyone who can help." Maybe expecting a satisfied nod or uttered greeting, she instead hollered as Juni swept her up into the air, swinging her around.

"Permission! Let's remember! Permission!"

Yet everyone was smiling as Juni set Dime back down, despite the indignity and wear on her pants of being shuffled side-to-side to make sure she was stable. "I'm fine, I'm fine, Juni. Thanks."

She ignored the smirk on Luja's face. "So, now what? I'm out of food, and I was going to go back to the hut, but you're not there anymore." *And you didn't want me to go with you to the Beds.* She understood vis logic, but she still felt strange about it. On multiple levels.

"Don't you have more pyrsi to talk to?" Luja asked. "You could still go back to the hut and rest and restock first. You'll know where to find us. I mean, we'll be at one of the two places, or at least we'd leave a note. And . . . you can fly, you know."

Yes, she could. And Luja was right; she needed to focus on the goal, fuzzy or not. "It's just hard knowing what the next step is," she admitted. "When they first appeared in our home, I was unprepared and confused, so I escaped. I was running, then surviving, then regrouping. Sometimes we do need to escape, but that's not the way to a solution, overall. It's pyrsi who care, talking, and working together, and causing other pyrsi to care. Being stronger together than the pyrsi who caused us to escape! It's clear to me now what we need—we need a coalition—dedicated to making our lives better. All of our lives."

And it was equally clear from Juni's warning there was even less time for that than she'd hoped.

"The answers won't all be there at the beginning. For example, could any Fo-ror move to Lodon? Would they have to use currency? Would the Heartland be more accommodating to pyrsi without wings? Or is that a cost of moving there?" She glanced at Stern Eyes and grimaced. "Home Sha will be a tough one to sort out. But at least we'll have pyrsi dedicated to talking. Dedicated to working through our issues in a way that considers everyone's needs."

"I hadn't thought about how much would be different," Luja mused, leaning back on vis hands. "It would be a new Ada-ji."

"No." Dime didn't mean to correct them so boldly, but she'd thought about this a lot. Since the beginning of this. "We can't think of it as a new world. This was always our world, and we chose to live in it this way. Collectively, at least. New friendships, new partnerships, changes in life, sure. But we've only had this one world, and as far as I know, we only will. Best time we started thinking of it that way. And I owe the newts an apology—I'd never considered them as part of it. Not enough. Tell them I'm glad they're here. I mean, what better ally have I had from the start of this than Juni?"

"Da-da," Tum answered.

Dime's head snapped around. *Of course, Dayn.* But he wasn't an ally, really. He was her spouse. That was closer. "You're absolutely right," she said. "I meant, outside our family."

Tum smiled, accepting the correction. As a bird sounded overhead, the four of them leaned back, and breathed in the winds and smells of the forest. Allowing herself, just for one more stride, to relax, she let her mind clear. It felt so nice to be here, talking with her children and friends.

So Dime didn't understand why Stern Eyes suddenly leapt to her feet, howling like a wind siren. Juni followed, not far behind, nearly barking.

"Tum!" Dime looked with alarm at her child, suddenly glad she had Volana's extra chair. Without her own chair, Tum could not move too quickly. She trusted the newts to carry her, but the chair was another option, for whatever was happening.

Understanding her meaning, Tum swung over to where the newts howled, making a series of grunts and howls herself. She gasped, turning back to Dime. "Bad two-legs! I mean, fairies! I mean, fairies are coming, and Stern Eyes says they're the mean ones. She's very upset."

"There!" a voice yelled.

Oh, Sol's auncle. Dime knew that voice.

"Everyone, don't trust these pyrsi no matter what they say. Don't talk, and find a way to leave. If we're separated, go to the Beds or the hut. Whatever is easiest." She nodded at Stern Eyes, making sure Juni could see her. "Bad! Bad two-legs! You're right!"

There were two fairies diving their way. One, as she knew, was Neimano. Beside him, the guard who'd tried to mislead her by taking her to Neimano's study instead of Ferala's. Tikinal had called xem Ulkanet, she knew from the takes she'd spent by the compost, rerunning the conversation in her mind.

She'd seen what Neimano could do, not just cycles ago but now as well. Her heart thumped, remembering the way he'd hurled some sort of force at her and Rock, how it had destroyed the beautiful statues instead. The memory spread, racing through her veins.

There was no easy way to flee. The fairies could fly faster than they could all walk, and even if Dime could manage to fly the whole group away somehow—even if she could, she wasn't sure she'd risk it with the newts—she'd have to tap deeper into her valence, which would leave Neimano and Ulkanet a distinct trail to follow. Even if she could get her children away, she wasn't leaving Juni and Stern Eyes here with these two.

Neimano landed a small distance from them, wincing with disgust at the newts, then smiling as he saw Luja and Tum. Familiar feelings gripped her, and all at once, she was sick of them. Done. No, she was not letting him intimidate her. She had enough to worry about between the masses who played with conflict to waste her energy on one disgusting pyr.

She'd protect her children and send him on his way. The Fo-ror would deal with him; they'd have to one way or the other.

Dime rolled her eyes as he strode forward. Not interested in some villainous entry, she went ahead and took it from him.

"Third Seat Neimano. How *interesting* to find you here."

He stopped a moment, searching for a response.

Heh. "Now I need you to leave," she continued. "You aren't welcome."

"Oh, we'll leave, alright."

Harm it, she thought she'd set the tone. "I know, you'll leave with us in tow. But no, we're not going. You really need to take the hint. So I'm asking you, pyr-to-pyr because certainly you have some decency left. You've seen I'm here with my children; please leave now."

"Give me my pendant and we'll discuss it."

She'd forgotten his obsession with the diamond. She waggled her fingers. "Who can own the stones of the world? It's around my neck, and I plan to keep it there."

"It's mine!" he snarled.

Watching his contorted scowl, Dime couldn't reconcile the idea of Neimano having given her this pendant. His resentment went deeper than her own betrayal, as he would see it. *Oh.* It clicked.

"The surgeon, you gave it to him, didn't you? A gift in exchange for his deeds? And," she considered, "probably only after you threatened him anyway. You thought the diamond would seal the deal, as they say. But he didn't want it. He didn't ask for it, and he knew it reflected the blood on his hands. I was the first one, wasn't I? He gave it to me. Without telling you."

Neimano's face gave her her answer.

"Then, certainly, no. It's not mine either, but I'm honoring his decision. He chose me over you, didn't he? Oh, that has to sting." Dime didn't mean to taunt, but the pyr daring to approach her children set her off pretty nicely. At least he'd learn she was serious.

"I'm not playing any more games with you, Diamond. Give me the pendant, and I'll be on my way."

"No," she said.

"Then you're coming with us this time, *without question,* and since no one is here to witness, we'll do this my way."

Dime looked past Neimano at the fairy behind him. "What about

High Guard Ulkanet? I bet xe's witnessed quite a lot. Maybe xe takes issue with threatening an innocent pyr having a nice talk with her children."

"And newts!" he spat.

Though Stern Eyes remained still, Juni growled, and Dime reached for her arm, stroking it. "Yes, and newts. They're my friends."

Neimano sneered, but kept his gaze focused on Dime. "Ulkanet does know a great deal." He didn't turn around but did swing an arm backward, in an awkward pointing gesture. "And I am confident the High Guard will say nothing." He laughed, a big laugh.

Dime's anger lessened, and she just felt such sorrow for a pyr whose best happiness was holding threats over others. How alone Neimano must be.

"We're leaving," she said to the group. "Stay with me."

Then, the breath tightened in her throat. A barrier of pressure surrounded her, no, all of them, by what she could tell. Able to breathe, barely, but otherwise immobile, she felt stunned. She tried to reach for her valence, but it felt trapped as well, pressed inside her. She was sure she could overcome the barrier, but it might take some thinking. And it wasn't as if she could drop into meditation with her children and friends unsafe around her. She couldn't talk, and she couldn't leave. Panic rose inside her, and with the only motion she had available, she stomped it down. No, this pyr did not control her.

As she reached and pried, not through motion but with her mind, she felt around for cracks in his barrier. She found them. She could pry it apart.

Then Ulkanet stepped forward with ropes. Glistening, diamond ropes. Her mind seized; she saw xem not here, but in her home, moving toward her, staring at her pendant. She withdrew again, into herself, the valence slipping.

No! She'd been through so much since then. She was not that pyr anymore. She was more now.

She braced for Ulkanet's approach. But xe stayed in place.

"Ulkanet," Neimano directed. "Oh, look, xe has no legs. You'll have to get creative, I suppose. We'll tie this one first."

Tum did not scream, not through bravery, but because, like Dime, she was held by the pressure of the air. Dime's breath drew tightly and with great effort; her heart pinching with terror for her children, she hoped with all her being that Tum and Luja could breathe. Juni and Stern Eyes also. But Tum. Sweet little Tum.

As Ulkanet approached the ch'pyr, Dime dug deep. Whatever she'd grasped before, she would find it. They would not tie Tum. *They would not.*

With a huge, fierce howl, Juni broke free and jumped forward, lifting her huge scaled arms up above Ulkanet's head and shoulders. From the side, Dime could barely see Stern Eyes, but she could sense her fear.

The barrier shifted, and changed, and all around her she was immersed in something she'd never felt *outside* of her body before: *anger*. Literal, genuine anger, tinged with a metallic sense, like it had been pressurized itself, more than the air Neimano had touched.

As Juni started to lurch, Stern Eyes burst forward, pushing Juni aside and releasing lines of pure silver sparks from her body, which bent and joined and rushed right at the two fairies.

As Neimano and Ulkanet dropped roughly to the ground, the pressure disappeared around them. Dime reached for her throat, turning immediately to Tum and Luja. Tum had fallen onto her side, and Luja waved Dime back, as if urging her not to turn away from their assailants.

Stern Eyes whipped around, her eyes still wide, and screamed in a host of tenors. Dime couldn't tell what was speech, what was regret, and what was anger and fear—it was a barrage of furious sounds. Juni stepped back, tripping over her own feet.

Then, as they watched her, Stern Eyes appeared to disappear in place, fading into the night. But she was not gone; Dime could hear the sounds of her rushing and stomping through the forest, trampling the underbrush without finesse.

Dime grasped what had just happened—she knew what she had seen, but she could not think, not now. She turned toward the fairies.

Neimano rose, his body twitching and shaking and eyes highly disoriented. Looking up and seeing Juni running toward him again, he launched into the air, spinning and weaving but making his way through the trees and quickly out of sight.

"Juni, come back," Dime urged. Tum followed her comment with something in newt and, visibly distraught, Juni lumbered back, sitting next to Tum and pulling her close. Small whimpering noises escaped her as Tum whispered something that sounded like comfort.

Ulkanet lay still, on the ground. Dime could see xe was breathing.

"Xe's alive," Dime said. "Xe's alive. Come, we need to go. Back to the Beds. Now. We can't stay here."

"We can't; xe's hurt!" Luja ran to get vis lamp then rushed over with it, lowering to vis knees beside the fairy. "It's not just the shock—xyr neck grazed this stump when xe fell." In the nightlight, Dime could see the jagged tree stump glimmering, with blood, she presumed. "We can't leave xem like this."

And so Dime waited, nervously watching the skies, as Luja took a small blade and cut strips from vis suit top, removed a balm from a small bag, and carefully began to treat the wound. All the while, ve checked breathing, changed the position of the fairy and xyr wings, and whispered to verself.

Behind her, Juni and Tum held each other close, murmuring in rhythms Dime couldn't understand.

Dime glanced back and forth between Luja's work and Tum's hushed conversation with Juni. It was dangerous to stay where Neimano had left them, and several times, she almost told Luja they needed to leave. Yet she held back.

Tum called to her mother, and Dime moved back to join them. She turned so she could keep an eye on Luja, training her eyes on Ulkanet's limp form.

"Juni says I can tell you more now. Lu, can xe hear us?"

"No, xe's out cold," Luja answered. "I'll let you know if xe wakes."

Still, Tum lowered her voice. "So, they aren't allowed to do that. No . . . hurtful emotions." Tum hesitated on her words, like saying *hurtful* could get her in trouble. Dime nodded her on, trying to reassure her. "Stern Eyes, when she left she was shouting that because of Juni, because of pyrsi, she'd lose her name. That the Violence would retake them, all because of us. Juni's not mad at Stern Eyes; she respects her a lot and feels bad she's scared. She thinks she should have acted sooner, to prevent Stern Eyes from doing what she did. She was scared to really . . . hurt him and so she hesitated."

Thinking back, Dime was pretty sure Stern Eyes acted specifically to keep Juni from doing anything. It had come across as protective. Parental. But she wasn't going to open that tin with Tum or Juni. Not here.

Juni whimpered.

"She says Stern Eyes saved you; she won't tell anyone. Stern Eyes doesn't need to worry about losing her name."

Dime rubbed her hands together, realizing they were trembling. "Tell her I'm sorry this happened. Ask her . . . how Stern Eyes can lose her name if she's the leader of their troop."

Tum conferred with Juni.

"She's the leader of their troop. But there are other troops. And newts are tied to something I can't understand."

"Probably their code of ethics," Dime murmured, no longer able to doubt the idea. Luja continued to work on Ulkanet. They needed to leave.

But Tum and Juni were now arguing, at least it seemed that way. Juni let little crying noises, then ran away from where they sat. Dime didn't pursue her; she could see her hiding in the trees, and knew Juni wouldn't leave Tum.

"I told her I had to tell the other part," Tum said, her voice sad. "The newts . . . they have valence." She whispered that last word.

"That's what that was. It's about how they feel. If they're mad enough they could even—" Tum hesitated.

"They could kill with it," Luja said, still hovering over Ulkanet. Dime wondered if ve was enhancing vis hearing. "I knew that the stride I felt it. It felt like anger. In the air. Ma-ma, you felt it right? How *much* anger she had."

"I did." Yes, that made sense. The newts, starving and freezing on the beaches, had had plenty of time to build up their emotions, bottle them in. And if their valence was emotion-based, then she could only imagine how powerful it could be. How dangerous. Her own hurt was minor compared to what they'd been through. And Dime had bent the land itself to protect her child. Yet the newts had showed restraint. Now what might they do? She shivered.

"Juni?"

The newt shuffled over, her head low.

Dime stood, leaning toward her. "I need your help. Can you take Tum back now? She's only a ch'pyr, and I don't want her here anymore." She glanced up into the sky.

Tum, making a face, didn't translate, but Juni seemed to understand Dime's tone and gestures.

Communicating briefly, Juni lifted Tum into her arms. She carried her first to Luja, who whispered in her ear, and then to Dime, who held her as close as she could, despite the tickle of Juni's feathers.

"Tum, tell Juni to talk to Stern Eyes. Tell her to calm her. Or do it yourself. Stern Eyes must feel very guilty. What happened here was not her fault. Tell her that. Tell her . . . we care about her. Ok?"

"I will, Ma-ma." Tum's eyes glowed with purpose, and Dime beamed with pride—a small lift to the weight of her worry—as Juni ran back off into the forest.

"Ma-ma!" Luja's voice called behind her.

Dime spun on her feet, rushing over, to see that Ulkanet was stirring. Xe sat up and Dime urged Luja back.

The fairy looked disoriented, stunned. It took xem a stride to understand where xe was, and Dime waited, wary. Xyr eyes opened with sudden recognition. "You can't stop us," xe said. "You have accelerated the inevitable."

"What?" Dime coaxed. "What is inevitable?"

"The curse. The curse will take you." Then, rising suddenly, xe stood. "We will prevail. Seat Neimano was always right. And we'll tell them. We'll tell them what you did here."

"Burge," Luja offered.

Ulkanet spun around, appearing surprised to see ver.

"Your eyes. You're not well. Can you rest longer? I promise I won't touch you again. We can leave."

Sputtering, the fairy lifted up, and like Neimano, zipped onto a labored, jagged path away from them.

It was just Luja and Dime now, standing in the dark forest lit only by the small, flickering lamp. Dime tried to make sense of what had happened, but it was difficult, with so many developments all at once. But she had been here before. She could cope with it. And Luja, she needed to make sure Luja was alright.

"Are you ok?"

"Yeah." Luja's gaze flitted about the trees, as if making sure they really were alone.

Dime noted the fabric torn from vis top; the Fo-ror blood staining vis sleeves. "About the newts," she started.

"Yeah. That's a lot."

"It is. I don't know what the Fo-ror will learn from this and we can't stop that."

"They both acted like they thought you did it."

Dime took that in. "I think you're right. Maybe that will protect the newts for now. We can't have word out amongst the Fo-ror; think what that would do to their resolve. And I hope the Circles don't find out, either. Can you imagine their reaction?"

"That the newts can be used for the Violence? Maybe just by inciting them a little, then hey, it wasn't our fault?" Luja raised vis nose. "Not interested in giving them that option."

She was stunned by the brutality of the idea, but, no, ve was right. That was a risk, especially with pyrsi feeling so threatened. Dime wondered what other angles she hadn't yet considered. "I agree. We'll have to keep it secret. If we can."

Luja looked at Dime as if she didn't see something. Something sad. "What? What is it?"

"I know I'm not as old as you. But I've learned a few things. And one thing I've learned is about secrets. They're like wounds. The bad part either finds a way out—or it kills you."

Dime tried not to react to the harsh language from the young mouth. Except, she meant it. And there was a solemnity in Luja's words that rang true. She was proud of ver. The air between them felt right, in that moment, and Luja was a separate, grown being. And Dime was so proud—*so proud*—to be vis mother.

"You're right, Buttons. We'll do what we can. Hey, I'll help you get back to the Beds. At least partway."

Luja shifted. "I can go by myself, if that's ok. You have more to do. I'll be ok. I promise."

Dime stood, hesitant. Could she really let her child walk off across the foreign Heartland, takes after they'd been, well, she had to say it, *attacked*? Or . . . could she not let ver? She knew that answer, though it pained her, deeper than her heart, even, to admit it.

"Ok. Stay safe? And make sure your father knows exactly what happened. The newts could be at risk if Neimano realizes that wasn't me."

Luja nodded.

"And the Fo-ror—" She hoped the newts wouldn't do anything drastic either. Dayn, he'd try to talk to them.

Dime couldn't take it anymore. She offered her arms for an embrace, which Luja accepted. "We're going to do this, ok? Tell your father—we're going to get pyrsi together and we'll talk this through. It may not be easy, but we'll do it. We're not backing down because some pyrsi want to scare us away . . . to protect what they know. Including what they keep. We won't stop. We'll do it together."

Together. She couldn't deny the image that formed in her mind. And somehow, she knew Luja would want to hear this too. "Hey. My friend, Rock? The one you said was secret? She's not. She's a good friend, and I'll find her. I need her too, just like I need you, ok? And if I've upset her, I'll apologize. I'll let her know."

Luja's worried grimace broke into a smile. "I think that's nice. I think you're nice. Well, anyway, we don't know if they'll come back, so we'd better go. Get away from here." Ve shrugged.

"Yeah, sure," Dime agreed, her heart aching to stay with her child. No matter how grown ve was, she was sure that instinct would never fade. Nor did she want it to. But, Luja was capable. Ve'd be alright.

"Bye, Buttons. I'll see you soon." She reached down and handed ver the lamp. "Tell your Da-da I love him and miss him."

"I will." Ve looked happier than before, then bowed vis head, eyes fixed on the ground. For a stride, Luja appeared to be searching for an appropriate farewell. Sighing, ve looked up. "Ma-ma," ve said, "I'm glad you're you."

Dime embraced her child again, not letting ver know how scared she was to send ver out, alone, into the night. But one thing bolstered her resolve.

Those were the best words she'd ever heard.

END OF PART 05

About the Author

E.D.E. Bell was born in the year of the fire dragon during a
Cleveland blizzard. After a youth in the mitten, an MSE in
Electrical Engineering from the University of Michigan, three
wonderful children, and nearly two decades in Northern Virginia
and Southwest Ohio developing technical intelligence strategy, she
now applies her magic to the creation of genre-bending fantasy
fiction in Ferndale, Michigan, where she is proud to be part of
the Detroit arts community. A passionate vegan and enthusiastic
denier of gender rules, she feels strongly about issues related to
human equality and animal compassion. She revels in garlic. She
loves cats and trees. You can follow her adventures at edebell.com.

Continue Dime's story in . . .

Part 06: Freedom

edebell.com/diamondsong

www.ingramcontent.com/pod-product-compliance
Lightning Source LLC
Chambersburg PA
CBHW032037180726
48284CB00008B/2630